W9-CHG-590

Other books by Paula Danziger

PAULA DANZIGER

Thames Doesn't Rhyme with James

PAPERSTAR

Penguin Putnam Books for Young Readers

ACKNOWLEDGMENTS

For exploring London with me:
the Hamilton Family, Aileen, Nancy, and Harriet;
the Evans Family, Greg, Gill, Daniel, and Isobel;
The Tapissier/Birch Family, Charlie, Mary, William, and Elinor;
The Glekin Family, Barry, Helen, Nikki, Sammy, Benjy, and Adam;
Ben Blair and Tanya Blair

For listening:
Gill Evans
Jana Hunter
Bruce Coville

For extraordinary makeup at the Theatre Museum:
Lucia Tsappis
Lynsey Pinset

To all the taxi drivers in London, who have been so helpful

Copyright © 1994 by Paula Danziger.
All rights reserved. This book, or parts thereof, may not be reproduced in any
form without permission in writing from the publisher. A PaperStar Book,
published in 1999 by Penguin Putnam Books for Young Readers,
345 Hudson Street, New York, NY 10014.
PaperStar is a registered trademark of The Putnam Berkley Group, Inc.
The PaperStar logo is a trademark of The Putnam Berkley Group, Inc.
Originally published in 1994 by G. P. Putnam's Sons.
Published simultaneously in Canada. Printed in the United States of America.
Library of Congress Cataloging-in-Publication Data
Danziger, Paula. 1944- Thames doesn't rhyme with James / Paula Danziger.
p. cm. Sequel to: Remember me to Harold Square.
Summary: While spending Christmas in London with her family, her boyfriend,
and his family, fifteen-year-old Kendra finds herself roaming the city in another
scavenger hunt, like the one in New York the previous summer.
[1. London (England)—Fiction. 2. Christmas—Fiction.] I. Title. PZ7.D2394Tg
1994 [Fic]—dc20 94-19903 CIP AC ISBN 0-698-11788-3
10 9 8 7 6 5 4 3 2 1

For Josh Danziger,
the youngest nephew,
who wasn't born when
Remember Me to Harold Square
was dedicated to the rest of the family. . . .
This is your book.

CHAPTER
ONE

My life is filled with "What-ifs."

What if I flunk my trigonometry test? I have enough trouble spelling *trigonometry*, let alone doing it.

What if my English teacher gives a pop quiz on *Moby Dick*, and asks questions like. . . . "What is the first line of the novel?"

a)   Call me Ishmael.   b)   Call me collect.
c)   This is a fishy tail.   d)   This is a very fishy tale.

What if Barton Bertelski asks me out again? For the last two months he has been asking me out. He's the most disgusting boy in the entire school. He's the one who started the Pimple Wall, which is just too disgusting to discuss.

What if the teachers give us so much homework over the winter vacation that I won't be able to go to England with my family and Frank and his family for Christmas, or I have to spend my entire time there studying school stuff and never be with Frank?

What if there are no letters from Frank for more than three days? Since he went back to Wisconsin, we've been writing to each other practically every day. What if letters from him just stop?

What if Frank has found another girlfriend now that he's back in Wisconsin?

What if his old girlfriend wants him back?

What if he goes back with her even though she dumped him last summer?

Those are just the present "What-ifs."

There are a lot of future "What-ifs."

What if something happens and my family can't go to London?

What if something happens and Frank and his parents can't go to London, like they get run over by a tractor or one of the cows on their farm gives them cowpox?

What if Frank's father gets cancer again? What if his remission ends and he dies?

What if Frank gets here and I find out, or he finds out, or both of us find out that he no longer cares for me?

What if he still does care, but we never have a chance to be alone because my father will act like Attila the Chaperone when we are in London?

Or what if we care so much when we see each other in London that our hearts will break when we have to separate and go back to our own states? I will be in a very sorry state if that happens.

What if my genius factoid little brother, O.K. (real name—Oscar), has to spend the whole time with Frank and me once we all finally get to London?

What if no one but me wants to go to all of the art museums? Since I want to major in art history someday, it's really important for me to go. What if no one else realizes how important this is to me?

What if Barton Bertelski follows me to London to ask me out and to start an English Pimple Wall?

What if scientists prove that worrying is genetic? Since I have a mother who is a worrier and a grandmother who was an even bigger worrier, does that mean I'm doomed to early membership in the Worriers' Hall of Fame?

What if people discover how much time I worry about What-if?

What if I stopped being such a worrier?

What if I stopped thinking about "What-ifs"?

What would I do with all that extra time?

I'd sure like to find out.

CHAPTER

TWO

"We wish you a merry Chrismoose, we wish you a merry Chrismoose and a happy no school," Teri Watson is singing, and wearing a pair of reindeer antlers.

The antlers were a present for Teri's dog, Joe Cocker-spaniel, but Joe shook them off and ran into another room.

So now Teri's wearing them and singing the same words over and over again.

"Those are reindeer antlers, not moose." Shannon laughs and puts tinsel on the tree.

"I know." Teri grins. "But it would sound really dumb to sing, "We wish you a merry Chrisdeer.""

"Not really." Bethany grins, touches her heart, and sighs. "I, for one, am totally willing to have a merry Chrisdear."

I groan.

My best friend is always madly in love with some guy.

Her latest is Christopher Bregman.

Bethany starts singing, "I wish you a merry Chris-dear," while Teri continues with "I wish you a merry Chrismoose."

Ama and Akousa harmonize.

Since I can't sing on tune, I keep saying "Do-wah. Do-wah. Do-wah."

Shannon starts singing "Winter Wonderland."

Continuing to sing, we all dance around the Christmas tree.

Joe Cockerspaniel comes back into the room and howls.

In walks Teri's six-year-old brother, Brian.

Shaking his head, he looks at us and says, "Girls."

I grab one of his hands.

Teri grabs his other hand.

He joins us in going around the tree.

So does Joe Cockerspaniel.

Mrs. Watson walks in, puts her hands on her hips and says, "I ask you, is this any way to trim the tree?"

Her hands get grabbed and she joins the circle.

The doorbell rings.

It's the pizza delivery.

Whenever we all get together for special occasions, we always have pizza.

It's been a tradition ever since the seven of us became friends.

We do lots of things with the rest of our class, but about five times a year we get together, just us.

Mr. and Mrs. Watson and Brian take their pizza into the kitchen, even though Brian begs to stay with us.

That's a tradition, too.

"Pizza with pepperoni." Teri opens a box.

"Veggie pizza." Ama opens the other box.

We each grab a piece.

I look around at the different pizza-eating techniques.

Ama and Akousa are eating theirs exactly the same way, with the pizza flat out.

Since they're twins, they do a lot of things the same— not everything, though, since they went to different camps last summer.

Now Ama is wearing her hair short, with beaded corn-rows, and Akousa's hair is long and wild-looking.

And a lot of other things changed too, but pizza-eating isn't one of them.

Bethany's rolled her pizza up and is taking bites out of it from the side.

Teri doesn't like the crust so she's using her teeth to sort of plow the cheese and sauce off. Then she leaves the nude crust on her plate. It's kind of disgusting-looking but we're used to it. She's been doing that since third grade.

Bonnie is eating her pizza very slowly. Ever since someone told her that you don't gain weight if you chew each piece one hundred times, she's been doing that.

Meals with Bonnie can last practically centuries.

Shannon is exactly the opposite.

She vacuums the pizza into her body.

"You know, Kendra," Teri puts down her crust, which has teeth ridges in it, "this summer when I was in France, there were two English kids in my study group . . . . . .

and they ate their pizza with knives and forks."

"I prefer pepperoni with mine." Bethany laughs and wipes some of the sauce off her chin.

"You are so lucky to be going to London." Shannon sighs. "For yet another vacation, I have to go to Montana to be with my father, my semiwicked stepmother, and the two rug rats, her lovely little brats. You get to go to England and see your boyfriend."

"And might I add, you are so lucky to have a boyfriend." Ama pretends to wipe a tear from her face.

"Having a boyfriend is not always so lucky." Akousa has just broken up with her boyfriend.

"And while we're making up your lucky list, add to it the fact that Frank's parents are paying for your tickets," Bonnie says, and then takes another tiny bite of her pizza.

I nod.

I am lucky.

Frank and I care about each other.

I'm going to London.

It would have been tough for my parents to take us all to London, but because of "Serendipity Summer," the New York City scavenger hunt that our parents made up for Frank, O.K., and me, we can all go. We did all the assigned things, went to the places, ate weird foods, looked up facts. Mr. and Mrs. Lee promised the trip as our prize because Frank stayed with us last summer when they went to Europe to try to save their marriage, which had been in deep trouble even before his father got sick.

So I am lucky. But it's not all luck. There were times that were not easy, like when Frank got upset when his old girlfriend sent him a break-up letter and he didn't want to come out of his room. There were also great times, like when we kissed for the first time.

"I am so jealous . . . . . London at Christmas. How romantic. How terrific." Bethany wipes pizza sauce off her chin.

"Jealous." Bonnie looks at her. "You, the daughter of a movie producer, who meets movie stars all the time."

"It'll be so boring . . . . . Christmas in New York." Bethany sighs.

"I'd love it." Shannon sighs too.

I think about how much fun it will be to spend Christmas in another country, especially since my family's staying with my aunt Judy and she's going to have a Christmas tree because the guy she's living with isn't Jewish.

My family's Jewish, so we celebrate Hanukah.

With Bethany, I get to celebrate Christmas.

With Ama and Akousa, I get to celebrate Kwanzaa.

I love the holidays.

Akousa says, "Just think, Kendra . . . by this time tomorrow night, you'll be on a plane on your way to London . . . . . lucky . . . . . and you're finally going to be able to spend some time with Frank without him having to keep the promise to his parents not to get involved with you."

"That really was a dumb promise. I can't believe the two of you were so goody-goody to follow it." Bonnie giggles. "Oooh, I can't wait to hear what happens."

I open my mouth to remind her of how Frank had a girlfriend in Wisconsin when he first came to New York and how he made that promise before he even met me . . . about how strict my parents, the dating police, have become. But they've already heard it.

"I'm just jealous that you get out of school two days early. You don't have to sit around class doing busy-work or taking exams that teachers just give to keep us in our seats," Ama says.

Akousa finishes her sentence, "You know that the teachers are just counting the days, hours, minutes, and seconds to get out of there, just like we are."

Someone knocks at the door.

The door opens.

It's Santa Claus.

Actually it's Mr. Watson, wearing the same Santa Claus suit that he's worn ever since we all were in kinder-garten.

Back then it was very big for him and he needed to pad it with a pillow. . . . but now he's kind of grown into it.

Brian is dressed as an elf.

Mrs. Watson, dressed as Mrs. Claus, passes out candy canes.

Mr. Santa Claus Watson sits down on a chair, pulling up another one right next to him.

In his pack are the presents that we all bought for each other.

The rule this year was that we couldn't spend more than $5.00 on each person . . . $30.00 altogether.

———

We made that rule since not all of us have a lot of money and some of us have to give a lot of presents.

That's just for this party.

Actually, Bethany and I get real presents for each other. We just don't give them to each other at this party.

My presents are all the same.

I made out IOU's for everyone.

The papers say, IOU A PRESENT FROM LONDON, CHOSEN ESPECIALLY FOR YOU . . . . . . MOST PROBABLY TACKY, BUT MAYBE NOT.

It's going to be so much fun to shop for presents for my friends in another country.

Then when I get back we can have another pizza party where I will give everybody their presents and we can find out what we each did on vacation.

"Ho . . . . . . Ho . . . . . . Ho." Mr. Watson really gets into his Santa Claus imitation.

Brian is wearing a pair of musical gloves that play "Rudolph the Red-Nosed Reindeer." The right-hand glove has a picture of Rudolph, with a bulb that lights up his nose.

The Watsons really get into Christmas.

We each go up to Mr. Santa Watson and sit in the chair next to him.

He goes "Ho, ho, ho. And what would you like for Christmas, little girl?"

Everyone gives their answers: A new Porsche. For Montana to fall into a volcano. (Bonnie asked for the car. Shannon asked for the disaster. Actually, I think if

Bonnie ever gets to drive a car, that would be a disaster.)
Two new speakers to go with their sound system. (Ama
asked for one, and Akousa the other.) Bethany wants a
part in one of her father's movies, and I say that what I
want is art books.

". . . . . . and especially a young man named Frank,"
Bonnie teases.

I just smile.

I can't tell them what I really want . . . . . more than
anything else . . . . and not just for Christmas.

I want my parents to treat me more like a grown-up,
to let me make some decisions on my own, to not be so
overprotective. I want to learn who I really am and what
I really want.

But I can't say that out loud, not even in front of my
friends.

After everyone has her turn with Santa, and Mrs.
Santa Watson hands them a candy cane, Mr. Santa Watson goes into his red sack and pulls out the presents that
we put there when we came into the house.

Then Mr. and Mrs. Claus and the elf leave.

Brian doesn't want to go but his parents make him.

That's a Christmas tradition, too.

My six presents are arranged in front of me.

We all take turns opening our presents.

All of the presents are opened. From Ama, I got a
glove for my right hand with a rhinestone ring on one of
the fingers. Akousa's gift is the glove for my left hand. It
has rhinestones sewn on it to look like a bracelet.

"What a HANDy gift." I put them on to show everyone.

Shannon shows off her new crystal earrings, a gift from Bonnie.

Bonnie's given me a little glitter address book, "to keep track of all the names and addresses of all those cute English guys you're going to meet."

"I don't want to meet any cute English guys. I just want to spend time with Frank," I remind her.

"Silly girl." Bonnie always likes to sound so much older than the rest of us, like she's seen much more, done much more.

Actually, she has.

Teri's gift is a set of stick-on body tattoos.

Bonnie comments on the places to put them.

From Bethany, I've gotten something that looks like a credit card but it's actually a telephone card.

Bethany and I love to talk on the phone. It's one of our hobbies.

She explains, "My dad brought this back for me to give to you after his trip to England. Put this into a special phone and we'll be able to talk for five minutes. . . . . . I want to hear about everything, the places you go, the people you meet, how good a kisser Frank is, how it's all working out. . . . . And promise that you'll write the first second that you can. I want to be kept totally, totally informed."

"And then she'll report back to us," Bonnie says.

The girls all look at me.

I just grin at them.

They start chanting, "Promise. Promise. Promise."

I promise.

I can't wait for the chance to have something to report.

CHAPTER

THREE

What a night.

What a plane trip.

It snowed and snowed and then there was more snow.

That's what happened in New York last night.

And then it snowed some more.

The plane was going to take off at 7:00 P.M. but it didn't.

The 9:00 P.M. plane didn't take off either.

So everyone on both planes, actually on all planes scheduled to leave Newark Airport, had to wait.

It was a nightmare . . . . only we were awake.

The airport was filled with people trying to get somewhere for Christmas and with people who were waiting to pick up people in planes who couldn't land.

The coffee shops and restaurants were overcrowded.

I sat there, chewing my nails, wondering where Frank and his family were, if they were safe.

The "What-ifs" came back.

What if they had a blizzard while they were driving to the airport, or what if their car drove into a snowdrift and they won't be found until the thaw?

What if the planes in Wisconsin never take off?

What if we all can't get to London in time for Christmas?

I tried to read.

I tried to go to sleep.

Trying to sleep while sitting on airport chairs was not easy.

In fact, it was impossible.

Finally, the snow stopped.

Everyone got on the plane.

The wings were de-iced.

The runways were cleared.

The wings were de-iced again.

The plane waited in line to take off.

And then finally, it did.

I stayed awake, concentrating on keeping the plane up in the air and thinking about Frank and hoping he was safe.

Now we've got our luggage. We've gone through customs at Heathrow Airport.

We've made a pit stop at the bathrooms.

I look at myself in the mirror and practically throw up.

I look tired.

My hair needs a transfusion of shampoo and conditioner.

My rumpled clothes, which I've had on for what feels like days, need to go to the dry cleaner.

My body feels that way too, even though I brushed my teeth on the plane.

"Almost there," my mother says, as we get ready to walk out of the doors into the main waiting room to meet Aunt Judy.

I haven't seen her in so long.

Because there's so much going on in her life, she hasn't visited us for over a year.

We go through the doors.

A lot of people are waiting.

I wonder if they've been here for a long time at this end, since we were supposed to be here at 7:00 A.M. and it's now 3:30 P.M.

O.K. yells, "There they are!"

I look to where he's pointing.

Aunt Judy's standing there, holding on to a bunch of helium balloons and a huge sign that says "Welcome. I love you."

And standing next to her, holding a bunch of flowers, is Frank.

CHAPTER
FOUR

I rush up to Frank.

He rushes up to me.

I drop my carry-on bag.

He hands me the flowers.

"Thanks." I look at him.

He grins.

My father goes over to Frank and shakes his hand.

It's almost as if he is blocking my way so that Frank and I can't kiss each other hello.

I wish everyone would go away so that Frank and I could really kiss each other.

I really want to be kissing and hugging Frank and having him kissing and hugging me.

Frank whispers in my ear, "I'm so glad to see you."

"Me too," I whisper back.

I can tell that he has put on aftershave lotion or something.

I remember that I need a shower, that I must smell like Eau de Airport.

Frank doesn't seem to notice.

"Thanks for the flowers." I really want to say, "Kiss me."

From the way that Frank is looking at me, I can tell that's what he wants to do.

"Kendra." My aunt Judy rushes up to me and gives me a major hug.

I hug her back.

Then we look at each other and grin.

Aunt Judy looks great.

She's wearing a long brown skirt with a beige sweater and a brown tunic.

Her long necklace is made up of round beads and she's got on earrings that have three hoops.

I wonder if she'll let me borrow some of her clothes and jewelry now that I've grown up more.

I wonder if she'd be willing to trade right now . . . so that I could wear her nice, clean, beautiful clothes and she could wear my grubby airplane outfit.

Somehow I doubt it.

I look over to see what Frank is doing.

He and O.K. are doing "boy hellos," punching each other on the arms and saying, "How ya doing? Long time no see." Then they start on their Three Stooges imitations, going "Nyuk. Nyuk."

I grin at them both.

"Where are your parents, Frank?" My mother looks around the airport.

Frank comes over and puts his arm around my waist.

"Our plane ended up getting here before yours. So they went to the hotel. I wanted to wait until you all got here so I got some clean clothes out of my suitcase, changed, and have been sitting in the coffee shop with Judy talking and waiting for you."

"And now," Aunt Judy says, "let's go home. We'll drop Frank off at his hotel first and then I'll take you to my new home, actually to Trevor's and my new home."

Trevor . . . . I can't wait to meet him.

Aunt Judy has been writing and talking to us about him for almost a year.

When we first made plans to go to London, she was living alone and just dating him.

Now they are living together in a big house, instead of another apartment, because he's got two kids who visit them a lot.

But they're with their mother this vacation, so we won't get to meet them.

I'm just as glad.

Who wants to spend vacation with two kids we don't even know, when I want to spend as much time as possible with Frank? It's bad enough having O.K. with us a lot because that was one of the scavenger-hunt rules . . . . All for One and One for All.

I don't want to think about what it would be like to have O.K. and two other younger kids around.

Aunt Judy goes over to a machine to pay and get her parking ticket stamped.

Frank whispers in my ear, "I can't wait 'til we can be alone."

"Me too." I grin, thinking about how when we get into the car, we can hold hands and sit really close to each other.

We all follow Aunt Judy out of the building, cross a road, and head into the parking lot.

"Parking lots here are called car parks," Aunt Judy says.

———

I stand there looking at and smelling my flowers.

My father asks Frank a lot of questions, about how his father is feeling, how his parents are, what time will they all be coming over to the house for dinner.

I wish my father would stop yammering away and give me a chance to talk to Frank.

I don't understand what's happened to my father. He used to be a perfectly nice, sometimes funny, fun father. Sure, he used to be a little embarrassing sometimes, like when he'd say to O.K. or me, "Come here. I want to whisper something in your ear." And then we'd go over and he would lick our ears. He doesn't do that now that we're older, but he's different somehow.

My mother says that I'm now just at a stage where I think parents are pains, but that's not totally true.

I think that my father is at a stage where he has turned into a giant pain.

I just want some time to talk with Frank.

My father keeps talking to Frank.

Finally, we get to Aunt Judy's van.

———

Once the luggage gets loaded into the back, we all start to get in.

Before I can follow Frank into the van, my father climbs into the seat next to Frank.

O.K. and I get into the back.

Frank turns around and shrugs as if to say, "What can I do?"

I make a funny face, pretending to be strangling myself with a rope.

My father is making me a crazy person.

It's not as if Frank and I have had a long-time, great romance, as if we're going to run off some place and do wild things. We're really just at the beginning, but my father won't even let it begin.

After Frank turns around again, I look at the identification bracelet on my wrist.

It's the one that he gave me when he left. On one side it says SERENDIPITY SUMMER. I turn it over and look at the inscription on the other side. In very small letters it says REMEMBER ME TO HAROLD SQUARE.

That makes me smile.

There's a place in New York called Herald Square. When Frank first came to visit, he thought that there was some guy named Harold Square.

Now, it's something we joke about.

In the letters that I've written to him, I've talked about how much fun it'll be to get to London and see Harold's English cousin, Trafalgar Square.

O.K. sits next to me reading a guidebook about London and telling us important facts.

———

27

"Did you know that London was first named Londinium by the Romans in 43 A.D.?" he asks.

"I wasn't around then," my father jokes.

Sometimes I wonder.

O.K. continues, "Then in 61 A.D., Queen Boudicca burnt down the city and killed everyone who lived there . . . . ."

My brother, the junior factoid. Sometimes I look at my brother and wonder where he came from.

Some kids collect baseball cards.

Some kids collect stamps and coins.

Some kids collect dust.

I have a ten-year-old brother who collects facts.

"Wow," O.K. says, "it's a good thing we didn't come here in the 1600s."

Frank laughs. "I must have been doing something else that century."

"Ha, ha." O.K. smiles. "In 1665 a plague killed off about 100,000 people and then in 1666, there was the Great Fire of London. I'm glad we missed it."

Aunt Judy says, "O.K., are you looking at those books to prepare for the London scavenger hunt?"

At exactly the same time, Frank, O.K., and I yell out, "What scavenger hunt?"

There's a moment of silence.

Then Aunt Judy says, "Oops. I didn't know it was a secret."

"A surprise, not a secret, Judy. We were going to tell them about it tonight," my father says. "Don't worry.

I'm sure that the kids are going to have as much fun with this hunt as they did with the one last summer."

The car is very quiet.

I am thinking about Serendipity Summer, the New York scavenger hunt . . . . how sometimes it was fun and sometimes it wasn't. The three of us had to stick together all the time and do a lot of things.

I bet that Frank and O.K. are thinking the same thing.

I bet that O.K. is hoping that sushi is not on the list again.

Aunt Judy stops the van at a red light and turns. "Good. I'm glad that it didn't ruin anything. I've already told Colin and Emma about the hunt and they're really looking forward to it."

"Colin and Emma?" Frank, O.K., and I yell out.

"Yes," she says, "Trevor's children. There's been a change in plans and they're going to be spending Christmas with us. Their grandmother in Connecticut got sick and their mother is flying out today to take care of her. They'll be at dinner tonight. There was no way to tell you ahead of time."

My mother says, "That's all right, Judy. I'm sure that the three original Serendipities will be glad to welcome two more."

Two more! I didn't even know that we were having another scavenger hunt. Now there are two more people coming.

I wonder how old Emma is.

"How old are Colin and Emma?" O.K. asks.

The light turns green.

Aunt Judy starts driving again. "Colin is ten."

"Yes!" O.K. raises his fist. "Someone my age. Yes."

"And Emma?" I imagine her being fifteen, tall, blonde, beautiful.

"She's eight," Aunt Judy informs me.

I want to raise my fist and yell "Yes," but decide against it.

Frank turns around and grins at me.

I grin back.

Serendipity Winter . . . . here we come . . . . ready or not.

CHAPTER

FIVE

A promise is a promise.

I know that if I don't write to Bethany immediately, she and the rest of the gang are going to give me a really rough time when I get back.

Anyway, I really want to talk to Bethany, but it's too early to use the phone card.

So I take out my notebook and write.

Dear Bethany,
  Hello, London. Cheerio, New York.
  No. . . . Not one tiny little O of breakfast cereal . . . . . Cheerio . . . . . as in an English good-bye, how are you, what's happening. I'm trying to learn to be bilingual. . . . Teri isn't the only person who can learn another language. . . . By the time I get back I'll be able to speak English and American. So far I've learned to say loo instead of bathroom, and puddings for

desserts. I've also learned that candy is called sweets.

Here's the news.

We finally got here.

And there's no snow.

I'm in my bedroom (well, not exactly my bedroom because I've got to share it . . . . . . no, not with whom you think but I'll explain in a little while).

It's supposed to be "put your clothes away and take a nap" time.

I've just put my clothes away (plus that dress you loaned me—the one you call "that little hot black number.") I can't wait to wear it.

I've tried to nap. Waiting for the plane . . . . . the five-hour time difference . . . . . . I should be asleep right now . . . . . but I'm too excited.

In just a few hours Frank and his parents will be coming here for dinner (they are staying at a nearby hotel).

I did get a chance to see him, though. He was at the airport waiting for me . . . . . with flowers!!!!!!!!!!!!!!!!!! He's just as cute as ever . . . . He's still almost six feet tall. His hair is still blond. . . . His eyes are even sky-bluer.

And I still look the same . . . . . brownish-red hair, blue eyes, a bust that seems to be growing ever so slightly. . . . the same Kendra Kaye.

That's the good news.

No snow.

Frank.

The chance to see London.

What more could a person ask for?

Not much . . . . but wait 'til you hear about the stuff that's happening that this person hasn't asked for.

We've only just gotten here and the "grown-downs" are at it already (I don't want to call them grown-ups because they are doing things that don't make me feel very "up").

Here's the list:

1. My father is being totally weird. It's like he doesn't want Frank and me to be any closer than a million miles. I don't get it. . . . He likes Frank. . . . He likes me. . . . He wasn't like this when I went out with Jeremy. . . .

2. Aunt Judy's almost-step children (I don't know what else to call them . . . . . the children of the man with whom she shares this house and her life . . . . . too long. . . . I'll just refer to them as Colin and Emma) . . . . anyway, their grandmother got sick and their mother had to go take care of her so the kids are here with us . . . . . I have to share my room with Emma, age 8. . . . She's not here yet . . . . . Trevor is going to pick them up after work . . . so I'll meet the Atkinson family then—Trevor, Emma, and Colin . . . . and did I tell you that they are going to be part of the scavenger hunt . . . . ?

3. The Scavenger Hunt ...... Yes ...... just when you thought it was safe to go out in the world .... my parents and the Lees are at it again ..... they've planned yet another hunt for us. . . . maybe this is also a phase that our parents are going through and they will outgrow this one, too. . . . I'm beginning to wonder, though .... anyway, this one is called "Serendipity Winter" ...... December 23 to January 1 ... that's really only ten days ..... and some of them get taken up by Christmas Eve, Christmas, and New Year's Day. I can't begin to imagine what they have planned for all of us.

I wish I could call you but we're not by a phone that uses a phone card .... and anyway, I bet that by the time I call, I'll have lots to report.

Merry Chrismoose ...... and a Happy Chrisdear .... Ho, Ho, Ho.

Love,
Kendra

There's a knock on the door.

"Kendra. It's me. Your favorite aunt, Judy. Your only Aunt Judy. May I come in?"

I nod.

She knocks again.

I realize that nodding when she's on the other side of

the closed door doesn't tell her much so I yell out, "Come in."

She enters, bringing in a vase with the flowers that Frank gave me. "It was very nice of you to offer to leave the flowers downstairs, but I bet you really want them up here. So I called Trevor and he's going to bring flowers home."

I nod. I only said to leave them downstairs because my father suggested that would be nice because Frank and his parents are coming to dinner and it would make the table look prettier.

It's good to see Aunt Judy again.

She really understands me. Even when I was little she treated me like a person, which is not the way every adult acts with children.

"So now both of us will have flowers from the men in our lives." She puts the vase on the dresser. "Your Frank is a very nice young man. I really enjoyed talking with him while we were waiting for the plane to land."

I smile, a lot. "Aunt Judy, he's not really MY Frank."

"He sure does like you a lot."

"Did he say that?" I motion for her to sit down on the bed with me.

"Well, not in so many words . . . . . after all, I'm the aunt. . . . but when he talks about you and about the summer, his face just lights up."

I have a vision of Frank's head being like a 100-watt lightbulb on top of his body, and I giggle.

"Really. He was so excited that he was going to see you."

"He is nice, isn't he?" I sigh. "And very cute. Sometimes I can't believe that he really likes me. I feel so lucky."

"Why not?" Aunt Judy pushes my hair out of my eyes. "You're nice, too . . . . . . and very cute . . . . and very smart . . . . . and you've got a good sense of humor . . . . . . and you've got a wonderful spirit of adventure. He's very lucky, too."

I sit there, think about Frank and how we are going to spend a whole week together, and I grin and grin and grin.

"You're my aunt. You have to say nice things about me."

"No," Aunt Judy shakes her head. "I don't HAVE to say nice things. When have you ever known me to say something I don't believe?"

I grin again.

"I can't wait for you and Trevor to meet," Aunt Judy says. "I've told him so much about you. And, Kendra, he's a wonderful man. I hope that you like him."

"If you like him so much, I will too." I smile at her.

She shrugs and laughs. "Not everyone that I've gone out with is a person you would like. I didn't like some of them very much after a while, but Trevor is special. We like each other. We respect each other and we love each other."

"That's great."

"And I've come to love his kids."

"Are they here a lot?"

She nods. "Trevor and his ex-wife share custody. . . .

so the kids are here a lot . . . . . . and since they go to my school, I see them every day. . . . They come into my classroom to say hello or we see each other in the halls."

"Trevor's English, right?" I look at her and she nods. "So how come they go to the American School in London?"

"Joan, their mother, is American. When she agreed to live in England, the compromise was that the kids would go to an American school. So they do . . . . . . lucky for me . . . . . otherwise I might never have met Trevor at a Back-to-School night. They'd been divorced for three years."

There's a knock on the door.

O.K. yells, "Are you two going to stop yakking in there?"

"Join us," Aunt Judy yells back.

"Geronimo!" O.K. opens the door, rushes in, and jumps on the bed.

"The parental units are downstairs finishing up the Great London Scavenger Hunt and they didn't want me there while they're doing it." O.K. flops down. "I suppose that you don't want me here either. . . . Sigh. Nobody loves me . . . . . I'm going to eat worms."

"I love you." Aunt Judy leans over and starts kissing him on his forehead, the top of his head, his ear.

I start tickling him.

"Yuck. Aunt Germs. Sister Crud." O.K. tries to push us away.

"Are you going to admit that people love you, that we

want you to be here?" Aunt Judy kisses him on the forehead again.

"Speak for yourself, Aunt Judy." I continue to tickle him.

O.K. grabs a pillow, hits me with it, and screams, "Wicked older sister. You wish you were an only child. You wish that I wasn't around when you were with Frank. You wish I wasn't around when you're with your friends."

I grab the pillow.

I hit him on the head with it.

"And now you're trying to concussion me." He's still laughing.

"Concussion is a noun, not a verb," I inform him, and start tickling him again.

"Stop!" he yells. "Stop tickling. Stop kissing. Stop correcting my grammar. I give up. You love me. You want me to be around all the time."

"No. No. No. I do NOT want you to be around all the time," I let him know, and then I whisper in his ear, "But I do love you . . . . like a brother."

"I am your brother." He sits up and grins.

Aunt Judy looks at both of us. "I'm so glad that you both are here. I've really missed you."

"And we're glad to be here."

Suddenly and loudly, there's a shout from downstairs. "WE'RE HOME!"

And it's time to meet the two new Serendipities . . . . . and their father.

CHAPTER

SIX

"Why was Henry the Eighth buried in Westminster Abbey?" Colin turns to O.K. and asks.

O.K., the factoid, thinks for a minute and then shakes his head. "Dunno."

"Because he was dead." Colin grins.

Everyone else groans . . . . . except for O.K., who hits his palm on his forehead and says, "Duh."

Both of the boys give each other high fives.

I guess dumb jokes are international and I guess that ten-year-old boys are always going to tell them.

"I know something about Westminster Abbey," O.K. volunteers. "It's not a joke, though. It's a real fact. . . . It is kind of funny, though."

"Tell us." Trevor smiles at him and puts some broccoli on O.K.'s plate.

I look at Trevor. He's got a great smile. Tall, he's got blondish, baldingish hair. He's got hazel eyes with these lines around them that sort of crinkle when he laughs.

He's kind of cute, for an older person. The best thing about him, though, is the way he looks at Aunt Judy . . . all lovey and caring.

I think that on a scale of one to ten, Trevor Atkinson is an eleven . . . . . . Of course, Frank is a twenty.

O.K. ignores the broccoli and tells a fact, which he always loves to do. "It's getting so crowded that when some people die and are buried there, they are buried standing up."

I think about that fact and wonder how they stay in place and don't fall forward. Are they bubble-wrapped or Krazy-Glued in place?

"That's a gruesome fact to share with us at the dinner table, young man," Mr. Lee says. "Why don't we change the subject, now?"

Everyone at the table looks at him.

Except for me. I look at Frank, who makes a face.

I remember Frank once writing to me about how much he hates it when his father says "Young man" in a certain tone of voice.

Now I know why.

It's not a nice sound.

Mr. Lee turns to Aunt Judy. "Judy, this is a wonderful meal. You must share the recipes with Evelyn."

Now it's Mrs. Lee's turn to make a face.

Frank has also told me how she hates to cook . . . . . and what an awful cook she is.

Everyone at the table is quiet for a minute.

I feel so bad for Frank. From his letters, I know how

bad it is at home, with his father trying to rule everything and his mother so unhappy. I know how Frank is always on edge, waiting for a fight.

It must be terrible to have parents who don't like each other.

Frank looks miserable.

I wish I could hug him.

I don't know why Mr. Lee acts like a bully, making everyone talk about what he wants to talk about.

Everyone was having a good time and O.K. was only sharing a fact with us.

I try to understand. . . . Mr. Lee almost died when he had cancer and the doctors still aren't sure how long he has left.

I guess if that were happening to me, I wouldn't want to hear about people standing up in coffins even though it is an interesting fact.

I only wish that Mr. Lee didn't use that awful tone of voice.

Suddenly everyone starts talking about the Yorkshire pudding.

That's not as interesting but it's something that Mr. Lee obviously doesn't mind as dinnertime conversation.

I, however, find it boring, so I spend the time looking around at everyone at the table.

Especially Frank . . . . . he's looking especially cute in denim pants, a denim jacket, and a light blue sweater.

His parents look a little dressed-up for what Aunt Judy said was going to be a casual dinner, but Frank's told me about how much they like to get dressed up and how they don't have a lot of opportunity to do so while living on the farm.

Trevor tells everyone about some of the disaster meals he cooked when he was first divorced.

Colin and Emma make gagging noises to show how awful the food was.

"He even ruined the Cheerios," Emma tells us.

Mrs. Lee laughs. "Even I haven't done that."

Frank nods.

"I put the box too close to the stove while I was making porridge . . . . . . and set fire to the box."

"Cheerios Flambé. Now that's a recipe I would like." Mrs. Lee laughs again.

Aunt Judy looks at Trevor and smiles a lot.

He smiles back at her a lot.

You can tell that they really love each other.

And he's so cute too.

And I hate to admit it but his kids are really cute, too.

I was all ready to dislike them because I didn't want to have to spend time with them, but they seem really nice.

I just wish that I didn't have to share my room with an eight-year-old girl.

O.K. seems perfectly happy to be sharing a room with Colin, but they're the same age and have the same sense of humor.

Colin has the cutest freckles and red hair.

Emma is just beautiful. She looks like a rosy-faced angel with long blonde/brown curly hair, long eyelashes. When she smiles, her look changes—partly because she is missing a front tooth and partly because you can see the mischief behind her eyes.

She really is adorable.

I start to pay attention to the conversation again.

I also look at Frank while I listen to what Trevor is saying.

And Frank looks at me.

There are eleven people at the dinner table.

I wish that there were only two.

Trevor starts talking about a guy at work who is a train spotter.

I can't believe it.

He says that there are people in England who travel all over the country and hang out at train stations, writing down the numbers on the trains that pass. "They're called train spotters."

"And they have a certain look. They all wear anoraks," Aunt Judy contributes.

Anoraks. It sounds like a group of people who starve themselves to stay thin . . . . . One anorexic . . . . . . many anoraks.

Aunt Judy explains that anoraks are a type of jacket, a kind of windbreaker.

Trevor says a little more about the guy from work and then he sums him up by saying, "He's one sandwich short of a picnic lunch."

I think that's a great way to describe someone.

Wait 'til I tell the gang back home about that.

"I know someone else who is one sandwich and a bag of potato chips short of a picnic lunch," O.K. says.

———

"Tell us." Trevor smiles at him.

"It's this guy who is always calling Kendra up. Barton Bertelski," O.K. tells everyone.

"O.K." I stare at him.

"Tell us," Frank says.

"O.K.," I repeat. "Mom. Dad. Make him stop."

O.K. continues, "I heard Bethany and Kendra talking about him one day. He started a pimple wall at school, in the boys' bathroom. When the boys have zits . . . . "

"Make him stop!" I yell. "This is gross."

"O.K.," my mom says softly.

O.K. can't seem to stop himself and quickly continues, "And all the boys go into this bathroom when they have zits, squeeze them and squirt them on the wall. Splat. They have competitions on who has squirted the highest, the biggest . . . . . "

"Splat." Colin giggles. "Splat. Splat. Splat."

"O.K. THAT IS ENOUGH. This is not dinner conversation." My mother sounds strict but I can see that she's trying not to smile.

I can also see Colin mouthing the word *splat*.

"That's disgusting," Mr. Lee says.

"And this is the guy who is always calling Kendra up?" Frank asks, smiling.

I could die of embarrassment.

Everyone is laughing or looking disgusted.

O.K. is going to regret this.

I don't know how, where, or when I'm going to get back at him . . . . . but he's going to be very sorry.

"Don't worry." O.K. looks at Frank. "Kendra won't go out with him."

I wonder if they bury people standing up at Westminster Abbey who are still alive.

"I think it's time to go over the scavenger hunt," Trevor says, changing the subject. "It's getting a little late for those of you with jet lag."

I look over at O.K., who has a clear case of brain lag.

He pretends to be squeezing an imaginary pimple.

I'm going to get him.

But first . . . . . the scavenger hunt.

CHAPTER
SEVEN

Alone at last." Frank comes up behind me, puts his arms around my waist and whispers in my ear. "Let me be Frank with you."

I giggle—first at his joke and then at the fact that he has whispered in my ear.

Having a father who first whispers in your ear and then licks it makes it hard for me to be "ear-whispered."

Frank continues, "Unless you want me to be Barton with you."

"Frank Lee, I don't want to hear one word about Barton Bertelski." I giggle again when I think about his name, Frank Lee, and the word *frankly*.

I turn around and we give each other a kiss.

It's the first time we've been alone since we've gotten to England. We're alone only because we volunteered to clear the table. No one else offered.

I definitely like it when he's being Frank with me.

My heart is pounding fast.

My knees feel weak.

I can hardly catch my breath.

This must be love . . . . . or jet lag.

We kiss again.

And again.

And again.

I don't think it's jet lag.

"Kendra. Frank. Hurry up. We're all waiting. Aren't those dishes in the dishwasher yet?" my father calls out.

We stop kissing.

We look at each other.

And we kiss again.

I kiss him.

He kisses back.

And then we separate.

Frank looks at me, touches my hair and then kisses me on the top of my head.

We stand there, just holding on to each other.

"I've missed you so much," he says. "Things have been really bad at home. My parents yell at each other all the time and when they're not yelling, they're not talking. They each say stuff like 'Frank, tell your father that dinner is ready,' and 'Frank, tell your mother that I'm not hungry,' and they're standing in front of each other. When they're with outsiders, they pretend that everything is all right. I can't stand it. I wish I could see you every day to talk to you."

"I wish that too." I hug him tightly.

"When it was really bad, I just kept thinking to myself 'Just hold on. . . . Soon you'll be seeing Kendra.' Thinking about that helped."

I look at Frank.

He looks so sad.

My father calls out again, "We're waiting."

I turn on the dishwasher and then Frank kisses me again.

I'm leaning against the turned-on dishwasher, and Frank, who is also turned-on, is leaning against me.

My father calls out, "It's getting late. Let's go over the scavenger hunt, and then the Lees have to go back to the hotel."

Back to the hotel, he said.

It dawns on me.

For the entire vacation, I will be staying one place and Frank will be staying another.

So he'll be with his parents and arriving at places with his parents.

I'll be with my family, my aunt, Trevor, Colin and Emma.

This is a plot to keep us apart.

This is a pain.

Something has to be done.

I'm not a little kid anymore.

Frank hasn't been a little kid for a long time, as his old girlfriend would tell you.

"Kendra. Frank." Everyone is yelling for us.

My father comes into the kitchen. "Kendra. Frank. In the other room. NOW."

Frank and I separate and look at my father.

Then we follow him into the living room.

Everyone is sitting on chairs, sofas, and the floor.

Frank and I sit down on the floor and hold hands.

O.K. claps his hands and says, "Attention. Attention. Attention. I've written a poem about our trip and the scavenger hunt."

Oh, no. I've heard O.K.'s poetry before. He may be a factoid genius but he is definitely no poet.

O.K. stands up and reads from a grubby-looking piece of paper.

SERENDIPITY WINTER by O.K. Kaye

Before, London and England were just names,
but now I'm here in a country filled with Lords,
    Ladies, and Dames;
Already, I've learned that football matches here
    are really soccer games.
I can't wait to see the places that are so fames.
So why don't we get a tour guide named James,
to take us to see all the sights, including the River
    Thames.

He bows and says, "Thank you. Thank you. Thank you," as if we are all applauding.

So we applaud.

And then the comments start.

"I really like that rhyme scheme . . . . . *a, a, a, a, a, a,*" my father the English teacher jokes. "Shakespeare, watch out."

"That's really a poem!" Frank grins.

"I just love the way you used the word *fames* so accurately." I shake my head and laugh.

"Thank you. Thank you. Thank you." O.K. bows again.

Trevor says, "O.K., I have to tell you something . . . . T-H-A-M-E-S is pronounced *tems,* as if it rhymes with *hems. Thames* doesn't rhyme with *James.*"

Ooops. I thought it did.

Obviously so did O.K.

"But there is a Thames (rhyming with James), Connecticut, isn't there?" Frank asks. "Some kid moved to my school from there and that's the way she pronounced it."

Trevor shrugs. "I don't know."

Aunt Judy says, "Yes, but that's not the way it's pronounced here."

I guess there are going to be a lot of things to learn here . . . or maybe even learn differently.

"Let's get this show on the road," my father says. "We'll go over the scavenger hunt rules tonight, and then tomorrow we'll all go out together and see a lot and get everyone acquainted with London."

Everyone, I think. Everyone means eleven people. We're going to look like a class excursion or a scout trip or something.

It's going to be a nightmare.

"Here." My mother passes out the scavenger-hunt papers.

My father starts reading aloud:

SCAVENGER HUNT

TO: the Original Serendipities, Frank, Kendra, and
      Oscar (a.k.a. O.K.) and the New Serendipities,
      Colin and Emma
RE: SERENDIPITY WINTER

Having successfully completed Serendipity Summer in New York, the three original Serendipities will be joined by the newest recruits in a splendiferous exploration of London.

Colin claps his hands. "This sounds like fun. Things are definitely getting better now."

I think about how he and Emma were supposed to be spending the holidays with their mother.

My father continues:

THE RULES

1. Don't forget . . . . . . serendipity means "the ability to make fortunate discoveries accidentally." . . . . . Be prepared to learn wonderful things (just don't have any accidents).
2. As before, you will all work on this together and stick together, no taking sides, no arguing with each other.
3. Because of the limited amount of time in London (and because of holiday restrictions), this scavenger hunt will not be as all-encompassing as Serendipity Summer.

4. As in the previous hunt, the Serendipities are to keep an accurate day-by-day log, showing that all of the requirements in the contract are met. At the end of each entry, each Serendipity will enter a comment about the day. Later, copies of the log will be given to each participant as a remembrance.
5. The Serendipities are to keep their own souvenir books.

My mother gives each of us a scrapbook.

I look at Frank and cross my eyes.

He looks at me and does the same.

O.K. says, "I know what I'm going to put in the book to start . . . . . my plane-ticket stub and the flight plan for the trip over. The attendant gave it to me."

"May I see it?" Colin asks.

"Sure." O.K. nods.

"Me too?" Emma asks quietly.

O.K. doesn't seem to hear her.

"Now," my father says, "let's move on to part one— the facts hunt."

"I'm good at this," Colin and O.K. say at the same time.

"So am I." Emma chews at her braid. "I know a lot, too."

Colin looks at his sister as if she is a real pain . . . . . kind of the way I look at O.K. sometimes.

Emma looks so sad.

I smile at her to show that I hear her and am glad that she is here.

She doesn't see me because she's looking at the floor and chewing on her braid.

Just as I open my mouth to say something to her, Frank gives me a little kiss on the back of my neck.

I turn from Emma and look at Frank.

I've never had my neck kissed in front of nine other people. In fact, I've never had my neck kissed quite like that before.

I guess that Frank is letting everyone know that his summer promise not to get involved with me is no longer valid.

"Everyone, pay attention," my father says, frowning. "It's getting late. We'll save the other sections for first thing tomorrow morning before we start our sightseeing."

"Early tomorrow morning?" I moan. "I'm so tired."

Everyone looks tired.

My father speaks a little louder. "Come on, everyone. We've only got one week here. Let's make the most of it."

Sometimes I think my father should have been a tour director or an army general.

Everyone groans.

"Come on, everyone. It'll be fun," Colin says.

"Groan," I say, putting my head on Frank's shoulder, pretending to be asleep.

Then Frank's father says, "Oh, all right, I'm willing to

give it a try. We should try to do everything we can. After all, life is not a dress rehearsal."

The younger kids look at Mr. Lee as if he makes no sense.

Mrs. Lee frowns at her husband and then looks away.

Frank holds my hand a little harder.

My father starts going over the facts list:

1. How far is London from New York City?
2. When distances from London are given, what landmark is used?

"I know where you measure from in New York," O.K. calls out. "Columbus Circle."

"I know in London. It's Charing Cross," Colin calls out.

They grin at each other.

3. Why was the landmark given that name?

The boys look at each other and shrug.

"I know," Emma says.

"I bet you don't." Colin makes a face at her.

"I do. But I'm not telling." Emma makes a face back at her brother.

"Remember, you are all to work together," Trevor says softly.

Emma sighs and says, "Tell that to them . . . . . Oh, okay. I learned this in school. Charing comes from the French. It means "beloved queen," and when King Edward the First's wife Eleanor died, they wanted to take her to London to bury her in Westminster Abbey and every place they rested the coffin on the trip was marked with a cross. Charing Cross was the last place the funeral procession stopped."

"You're making that up. Why didn't they just fly her to London?" O.K. questions.

"It was a long time ago . . . . . 1291," my father tells them and then continues with the questions.

4. What does Soho mean?

"In New York, it's the area south of Houston Street. Do you have a Houston Street here?" I ask.
Everyone shrugs.

5. Where is Cleopatra's Needle?

"In Cleopatra's haystack?" Frank jokes.
My father continues with the question, ". . . and what is buried underneath it?"

6. Why are there blue plaques on some of London's buildings?

"Because they haven't brushed their teeth," O.K. jokes.
"Plaques, not plaque." Colin laughs. "The plaques show where famous people have lived."

"And you have to name ten plaques that show where famous Americans lived."

"Will there be a plaque on this house to show that we stayed here?" I ask.

"I'll put one up tomorrow," Trevor kids.

Mr. Lee interrupts, "Let's just go through the quiz quickly. I'm beginning to fade. Jet lag really gets to me."

He does look tired.

I hope that he's not getting sick again.

My father continues:

7. How did the area called Piccadilly get its name?

8. What is Big Ben, and give at least five facts about it.

9. What are the boroughs in Central London?

10. How is English time measured, and from where?

11. What are the Yeoman Warders who guard the Tower called? (Multiple choice . . . . . . Tuna Eaters, Chicken Eaters, Beef Eaters.)

12. Number 10 Downing Street is the official home of the Prime Minister. What is Eleven Downing Street? What is Twelve Downing Street? Who is Downing Street named after?

13. True or False. Explain your answer:
    The Cabinet War Rooms are where people go to fight about what kind of storage to put in their houses.

14. Are the Houses of Parliament real houses? Are they apartments (flats in England)? Explain.

15. True or False: The Royal Mews is where the monarch's cats are sheltered.
16. What flies over the east front of Buckingham Palace when the monarch is in residence? Is it the bluebird of happiness, a swarm of bees, or the royal standard?
17. Who was the Tate Gallery named after?
18. How did Covent Garden get its name?
19. Why are the Buckingham Palace guards' jackets red?
20. What is Speakers' Corner? Where is it?
21. How is English currency different from American currency?

"Do you mean electricity or money?" O.K. grins.

"Currency. Not current." Mr. Lee sounds so impatient.

Colin tries to make a joke about it. "I've always thought that talking about money was an electrically charged issue."

Groans from the groan-ups . . . . Even Mr. Lee smiles slightly.

My father continues:

22. What is a subway in England? How does that differ from subways in New York City, and what is the London underground transportation called?

"And the last question is . . . ." my father says, with a dramatic flourish.

"Last question. Thank goodness," Mr. Lee says.

My father continues, "The last question is, 'Why do people in London have to pay for a television license?' "

"You need a license to have a television?" O.K. is astonished.

Actually I'm pretty surprised also.

I know that people have to have licenses for potentially dangerous things like guns . . . . . . dogs . . . . . . marriages . . . . . . but for television!

Mr. Lee stands up. "It's time to go. Thank you so much for your hospitality. I'm sure that we are all very tired so . . . . . . until tomorrow."

Frank and I look at each other.

Until tomorrow.

CHAPTER

EIGHT

I'm in love. . . .

. . . . . Totally, completely, absolutely, and forever in love.

I'm in love with London.

I can't decide if I love the place so much because Frank is here with me or if I'd love the place no matter what.

Maybe if Barton Bertelski were here with me, I wouldn't love London so much.

He'd probably turn the front of Buckingham Palace into the Pimple Gate.

But Barton Bertelski isn't here.

Frank is.

That makes me very happy.

How can I be anything but happy with Frank? He keeps telling me how much he's missed me, how beautiful I am, and how much he loves me.

How can I be anything but unhappy with our families, who don't give Frank and me a moment alone?

At the moment, we are all standing around in the middle of Trafalgar Square, talking, and watching people feed the pigeons.

We just got back from a bus tour, which gave us a chance to, as my father says, "get an overview of the cornucopia of riches that is London."

Now that we have the overview, I wish that our families would leave and let the Serendipities get on with the rest of the viewing (I would really like it if they would leave Frank and me alone but if not, at least let us be the grown-ups in the group).

O.K. and Colin are holding a contest to see who spots a pigeon dropping a load on someone's head. They are calling the competition, "Spot the Spotter," and themselves "Pigeon Untrained Spotters."

"You should ask for anoraks for Christmas. That would protect you from pigeon poop," Trevor grins.

Colin and O.K. start to laugh and say, "Pigeon poop" over and over again.

Emma joins in.

It's so embarrassing and gets more embarrassing when O.K. and Colin start pretending to be pigeons, flying, dive-bombing, and pretending to leave pigeon droppings.

My brain is beginning to hurt from trying to mentally stop the boys from doing their birdbrained actions.

My brain also hurts from trying to think of polite ways to get the non-Serendipity people to leave.

I try. "Well, Mom, Dad, Aunt Judy, Trevor, Mr. and Mrs. Lee, it was really great to see all of those buildings while we were on the bus. It's going to be great to see them up close."

My mother says to everyone, "Do you think this is a good idea? Maybe I should go with the kids."

"We can take care of ourselves," Frank, O.K., Colin, Emma, and I say at almost exactly the same time.

My father sighs. "It'll be fine. We've given the kids instructions, phone cards, money, pieces of paper with Judy's address and phone number on them . . . . . ."

"We already know that," Colin says. "We'll be fine. My dad and mum let us ride the buses by ourselves."

"As long as you stick together." Trevor looks serious.

It's so embarrassing to have to go through this.

My father looks at his watch. "Kids, just promise that you'll be careful. I've got to get over to the Reading Room at the British Museum to do some research for one of my classes."

We all promise.

"And I have to go to my office for a couple of hours to clear my desk," Trevor says.

Mr. Lee yawns. "Jet lag really gets to me. I'm going back to the hotel to nap."

"Do you feel all right?" Mrs. Lee asks him.

"Stop worrying." Mr. Lee makes a face. "I'm just tired."

Mrs. Lee looks tired too. "Well, then, I'll go over to Harrods and get some last-minute shopping done."

"And I'm going back to the house to do some holiday cooking." Aunt Judy turns to my mother. "And, big sister, I thought you were going to help me."

With all of this talk about going, I wish that they would actually leave.

"Are you sure that you're going to be all right?" My mother looks at us.

"Mom. Everyone. Please. We'll be fine," I say.

"Pigeon poop!" O.K. yells. "I win. Look over there. One of them got a direct hit on that lady. Poop. Poop. Poop. Poop."

We all look at a very embarrassed, disgusted-looking lady who is standing there with bird droppings in her hair.

"O.K., stop that. Kendra . . . . . the Handi Wipes." My mother holds out her hand.

I open the knapsack she gave me this morning. It's filled with all sorts of supplies: maps, phone numbers, Band-Aids. I pull out the Handi Wipes.

My mother goes over to help the lady.

"Go quickly," my father motions to us.

We move quickly.

As we continue rushing away, my mother yells out, "Don't forget, they drive in the opposite direction than we do. Look both ways before you cross."

Crossing the street, we look both ways and head up the steps to the National Portrait Gallery.

O.K. and Colin race up.

Emma runs up behind them.

Frank and I walk up slowly, holding hands.

Moving my hand up to his lips, Frank kisses my hand.

It's so romantic.

"What took you so long?" The three kids are waiting at the top of the stairs.

That's not so romantic . . . having three chaperones. But that's the way it is, so I pay the admissions for everyone, since I was put in charge of the money.

In we go.

It's an amazing place, filled with all sorts of pictures of people.

There are portraits all over.

On the floor there's a mosaic of Greta Garbo, this old-time beautiful movie star.

Some of the artists are so famous and so are some of the people in the portraits. There are kings and queens and rock stars.

I love it.

I just know that someday I will work in a museum.

O.K. and Colin walk around saying "Boring," every three minutes.

"They are such babies." Emma puts her hand in my other hand, the one not being held by Frank.

"Boring." The boys race ahead.

I stop to look at some more of the paintings.

Frank, who is still holding my hand, tugs at it to try to get me to move faster.

I don't want to move faster.

"Do you really like all of this stuff?"

I nod.

"Are you going to take this long at each picture, in each museum?"

I don't know what to say, what to feel.

I want to say, "Yes. I am," but don't.

"The National Gallery is next door. Let's go through this one and then that one quickly and then we'll have time to have fun."

This IS fun, I think.

But again, I say nothing.

There are five of us here and I don't think it's right to make everyone else spend a lot of time looking at stuff they don't want to . . . . . . even if I do.

So I rush through the two museums. "Speed looking," I think it should be called.

I could have spent hours in the museums.

Standing outside the National Gallery, Colin says, "Let's go over to Covent Garden. It's so much fun."

Emma, who is still holding my hand, agrees. "There's a lot of outdoor shopping, Kendra. Didn't you say that you wanted to buy presents for your friends? That'll be a great place to do it. And there are some museums there . . . . . . fun museums."

"Do *fun* and *museums* go together?" Colin sighs.

"Nah." O.K. shakes his head.

I would like to do something awful to both of them, but they would probably use their phone cards to call home and rat on me.

So I just say, "And I hope we can spend a little more time at those museums."

"And we can watch people busk," Emma tells me.

"Busk?" Frank jokes. "Is that like pretending to be transportation? Cars, trains, and busks . . . . . "

Emma grins at him. "No, busking is people singing, playing music, juggling and stuff."

He grins back at her.

I think she's in love with him.

It's a good thing she's only eight.

"We can walk there or take the tube," Colin tells us.

"Our first tube." I make the choice and smile.

"I'll show you where to get it."

As we walk to the station, Frank puts his arm around my waist and says, "This will be fun. Don't be upset because we rushed through those museums. There's so much on the list to do. And you have to admit, some of those pictures were boring."

I pout.

Then he kisses me on the top of my head and then on my lips.

I unpout.

If Olympic medals are ever given out for walking and kissing at the same time, Frank could win a gold one.

If I keep "training" like this, soon we can enter as a couple in the synchronized walking and kissing competition.

"Want to busk?" Frank ruffles my hair.

"No performing in public places." I laugh.

"Shucks."

We walk toward the tube.

I decide to forgive him for making me rush through the museums.

Since I never told him out loud just how angry I really was, I decide to forgive him without saying a word.

We get to the station and use our transportation passes to electronically enter.

We go down steps, escalators, and elevators until we reach the train platform.

It's so clean, not like New York subways.

It seems very deep down in the ground, too.

Quickly we get into the train, and quickly we arrive at our destination.

We get off the train, come out of the station.

Crowds of people, lots of shops and outdoor markets . . . . . . Covent Garden . . . .

The Serendipity Five have arrived.

CHAPTER
NINE

Ta, da!" O.K. looks up from his guidebook and points to the area in front of us. "The pizza at Covent Garden."

I look around. "Where? I don't see a pizza place."

Colin and Emma giggle.

O.K. hits his head with the palm of his hand. "Duh. It's the Piazza, Pea-ah-za, at Covent Garden. I must have read it wrong . . . . not . . . . Kendra, you are so gullible."

"Gullible's Travels." I grin. "We read that in English class."

Frank gives me a hug and kisses me on the top of my head. "Gullible, but cute."

O.K. continues, "*Piazza*. The word comes from the Italian and it means an open public square, especially one surrounded by buildings."

I look around. On the left are open stalls selling all kinds of stuff like leather bags, antiques, towels.

On the right are stores and a restaurant.

Straight ahead there is a long group of stores with a path through one section, which must be the Piazza.

I walk toward a stall that interests me.

"Boring!" O.K. and Colin say at the same time.

I'm beginning to think of them as the "Boring Twins."

"Are you going to shop all the time?" Frank puts his arm around my waist and kisses me on the forehead. "Colin says that there is usually some really good busking through the next set of buildings."

"Why don't you take them over there and I'll meet up with you in a few minutes?" I suggest, frowning.

"I want to spend every minute with you." He kisses me on the back of my neck.

I pick up two tiny leather pouches that I know Ama and Akousa will love, and pay for them.

"All done?"

But he's not really just asking because he's sort of leading me out of the stall area back into the crowd.

We walk for a few minutes.

There are so many places where I want to stop, shop, and look.

Emma points out a couple of her favorite stores.

"Are there any stores here that sell old music?" Frank asks. "My parents bought me an old jukebox for Christmas and I want to find some old forty-fives."

"What are old forty-fives?" Colin wants to know.

"Middle-aged people." I giggle.

Frank laughs and explains, "Old-time music records like from the 1950s—rock 'n' roll is what I want."

"No record stores in the Piazza," O.K. informs him, "but we could get you a roll from the food section . . . . . and we can find a rock on the ground somewhere."

Frank starts doing a Three Stooges imitation.

Emma points. "Look at that."

On the side of the Piazza, a busker is organizing the crowd to cheer, applaud, and yell when he does his next trick.

"Now for the London Transport Museum." O.K. looks at his list.

"Museum," Frank says. "You'll like that, Kendra."

I wonder. I wonder if I'll like it. I wonder if he's being sarcastic but then he kisses me on the back of my neck and I stop wondering.

We continue walking through another set of archways.

There are more stores, more stalls, and an amusement area with rides and games of chance.

"This isn't here all the time," Emma informs me. "It's only here on some special occasions."

The Boring Twins aren't so bored anymore.

They beg to go on the rides.

When I say "No," O.K. looks at me, squeezes at his face, and goes "Splat. Splat. Splat."

Colin joins in.

Frank laughs.

If they think that reminding me about Barton Bertelski and his stupid pimple wall is going to put me in a good mood and make me say yes, they have another think coming.

"No, you can't go on rides right now." I stamp my

foot. "You can do that anytime. We have to do the Serendipity Winter stuff now, and stop that splatting."

"Rides like that in the middle of New York City?" O.K. makes a face. "Come on, Kendra. You know that's not true, and anyway, you're not the boss."

"The London Transport Museum is on our list. Bumper cars aren't." I stamp my foot again.

"Temper. Temper." O.K. shakes his finger at me.

"Temper. Temper." Colin does the same.

"Come on, guys, let's go to the museum and then if we're all on good behavior, maybe Kendra will let us go on some of the rides."

I stare at Frank Lee, the guy whom I have thought about almost nonstop since he went back to Wisconsin . . . the guy I practically dream about, the guy who gave me the I.D. bracelet that I never ever take off.

I look at cute, sweet, wonderful Frank Lee, and want to scream.

And I am angry.

I am angry at Frank.

I am angry at the Boring Twins.

I am angry at my parents, the Lees, Aunt Judy, and Trevor for this stupid scavenger hunt.

And this is only the first day of the hunt.

Here we are in London, in Covent Garden, and I'm ready to have a great time and I can't.

I stare at all of them. "Maybe we should split up."

Frank looks at me. "Split up?"

I nod. "Not you and me . . . . . not that kind of splitting

up . . . not right now anyway . . . but all of us go in different directions."

"One for all . . . all for one. Those are the rules," O.K. says. "Are you saying that we should break them?"

I think about it.

We're in a foreign city.

We've made promises to our families.

I don't feel sure enough of myself to go out on my own.

And there are two ten-year-old boys and an eight-year-old girl to watch . . . . . even though Colin and Emma know more about the city than I do.

Carolers start singing, "Peace on earth, good will to men."

Frank tries to make a joke. "They're playing our song."

I try not to smile.

O.K. says, "We don't have to go on the rides."

I look at everyone. "Let's go to the two museums here. And then we'll all go home and rest a little before tonight."

Everybody nods.

As we walk, I hear Colin say to O.K., "And I thought having a little sister was a pain in the neck."

When O.K. doesn't defend me and say that I'm a terrific big sister, I want to give him a real pain in the neck.

Emma walks up to them.

I don't know what they've said to her but she comes back to Frank and me.

"Emma," he says, "would you mind going up there with the boys? I need to talk to Kendra alone for a few minutes."

She sighs and walks behind the boys and in front of Frank and me.

"Are you all right, Kendra? What's happening? I've really missed you. I don't want you to be mad at me."

I say nothing.

"I wish we had some time alone, together."

I still say nothing.

"Kendra, talk to me. I hate this."

I look at him. "This summer we went to museums and you didn't complain. You didn't rush me through everything."

Frank looks down at the ground and then up at me. "I'm sorry. It was a long trip. And we've had no time to take it easy and I feel like we're babysitters. This is NOT my idea of a vacation."

I nod. "I know. It's hard. There's so much to do and so little time. And it makes sense that we go to all of these things together. It could be worse. Could you imagine what it would be like if our parents were on the tour with us?"

Frank takes a deep breath and crosses his eyes.

"I do like Colin and Emma—well, Emma at least— and usually Colin. He's good company for O.K., and O.K. doesn't have to hang around so close to us the way he did in New York."

Frank turns his head and looks at Emma.

"I feel sorry for her," I whisper. "The Boring Twins are sticking together and we have each other."

"We do?" He smiles. "We still do?"

"Yes. I guess we do." I give him a little kiss on his mouth.

And then it's more practicing for the Kissing and Walking Olympics medal.

"We're here," O.K. says.

The London Transport Museum.

We buy our tickets and go in.

It's actually interesting if you like trains, buses, and the Underground . . . . . horse buses and trams, steam undergrounds, transportation.

The boys are having a great time . . . . . getting on and off cars, playing with exhibits.

I, however, am not interested.

This is not a museum I would want to work in.

Obviously a lot of people here are having a great time.

I, however, am not one of them.

"Frank, what if you stay with the boys, and Emma and I go and do some shopping for a while?"

"One for all. All for one." He smiles.

"I want to pick up one or two more presents for you." I grin back.

"It's a deal." He gives me a kiss. "Let's meet up in front of the museum in about half an hour."

"Forty-five minutes."

I go over to Emma and whisper, "Want to go shopping with me?"

Her grin is so big it looks like it's going to fill her face.

As we go through the museum gift shop, I see the perfect present for O.K. It's called the London Game and the board is a map of the Underground system with the lines on it . . . Bakerloo, Central, Circle, District, Jubilee, Metropolitan, Northern, Piccadilly, and Victoria. The game cards tell about all of the places to visit and the nearby stations. The little factoid is going to love this.

I also buy some terrific postcards.

This is a museum where I like the shop better than the place.

We go back into the Piazza.

On the way, we look at some of the stalls and I buy a few more things . . . a macramé bracelet for Emma (I make her turn her back while I pick one out) . . . a black macramé choker with beads for me . . . . . and a leather bracelet for Shannon.

There's a stall that's filled with clocks.

I find a gift for Trevor, a clock that has a chalk-board face, with colored chalk to draw numbers and pictures on.

For Frank, I buy a clock made out of an old record, a really old record—a 78, a real antique. I bet it will look great next to his jukebox. I hope he loves it.

The Piazza is so crowded with people running around, buying last-minute presents.

We work our way back to the Transport Museum and meet the guys.

Frank's holding a little stuffed animal that he won at the carnival.

Obviously, they did not spend the entire time at the Transport Museum.

He gives me the stuffed animal, a teddy bear with a heart that says LONDON.

"There's a really great place that I want to show everyone." Colin points.

I look at my watch. "We have to go to the Theatre Museum. Do we have time?"

Colin nods. "You'll like it, too. I promise."

Somehow I think Colin would say that no matter what, but I figure, "Why not?" and we follow Colin downstairs.

"Stop!" I yell, spotting something in the window of a store. "I've found just the present for Bethany."

"Her best friend," O.K. explains.

I rush into the store and come out with a lace place mat of Buckingham Palace.

"That's gross," O.K. groans.

Everyone agrees.

"Bethany will love it." O.K. grins.

I agree.

O.K. knows that Bethany and I always try to buy tacky souvenirs for each other.

The Serendipities continue on.

The Cabaret Mechanical Theatre.

Colin is right.

It's a great place.

Getting our admission tickets, we put them in front of a mechanical man who stamps them. Inside, there are all sorts of handmade, hand-painted wooden and metal things with buttons to push, handles to crank and things move.

I push the button on one of them and a man in a bathtub filled with spaghetti starts moving the fork in his hand and "eating" the food.

It's making me hungry.

I'm beginning to wish that we really were in the middle of the Pizza at Covent Garden, not the Piazza. I know that we're having a great Christmas Eve dinner in a few hours, but I'm hungry now . . . . . A bathtub filled with spaghetti . . . . . or pizza. . . . is sounding very good.

"Kendra," Frank calls out, "look at this one."

I go over to where he is standing.

Colin, O.K., and Emma are next to him, in a line.

Frank pretends to crank a lever.

The kids pretend to be a mechanical chorus line.

They kick to the right.

They kick to the left.

They are all in unison.

Then the three of them pretend to pick their noses, all in unison.

I try not to laugh but I can't stop myself.

I am having such a good time.

And we haven't even gotten to the Theatre Museum yet.

CHAPTER

TEN

I got a spanking for doing this when I was little. I can't believe this is in a museum," O.K. says as we walk down a hallway.

It looks like a lot of people got into fingerpaints and left their handprints all over the walls.

What it turns out to be are handprints of famous actors and actresses.

I don't know a lot of the names next to the prints, but it is still fun to look at.

Maybe I should show a picture of this to Barton Bertelski.

A handprint wall is a lot less gross than a pimple wall.

Frank and I put our hands over the prints on the walls and then we hold each other's hands. We do that a lot.

Emma grabs my other hand. She does that a lot.

We walk through the museum.

All of the exhibits have to do with the theater, not really a surprise since we are in the Theatre Museum.

There are playbills, props, costumes, and pictures of famous actors and actresses.

"Hey, look at this," O.K. calls out, pointing to an exhibit called "The Perils of Powder and Paint."

It says:

ROUGE—Highly toxic, and a number of young beauties died from its use.

In 1864, the opera singer Zelger died of lead poisoning from a whitener used on his beard and moustache.

"Yuck," Emma says.

"Cool," O.K. says.

"O.K." I don't believe him sometimes.

"Hair today, gone tomorrow," Frank says.

"You are disgusting." I look at my boyfriend and then at my brother.

They give each other high fives. "Thank you. Thank you."

I decide to walk away from them, pretending that they're invisible.

O.K., Colin . . . . and Frank just keep laughing.

"They are so immature, those boys. Aren't they?" Emma says.

She looks so serious . . . . and so cute . . . . . . and so little that it seems funny that she's talking about people who are two years older and over seven years older than she is.

But she's right.

"Look at this." Emma points to a sign that says:

NOW IT'S
YOUR TURN TO
SLAP IT ON

_____

MAKEUP ROOM
OPEN TO ALL

"Let's go in."

The boys catch up with us.

"What if I get poisoned from the makeup?" O.K. says.

I just glare at him and don't say what I'm thinking.

He pretends to die on the floor.

"Be good," I warn them.

We enter.

A woman is sitting at a row of makeup mirrors with lights all around them, putting something on a little boy's hand.

It's a make-believe scar.

"That's great." O.K. looks at it. "Can I have one next?"

I punch his arm. "Say please. And wait your turn."

He looks at me. "I am waiting."

And then he looks at the makeup artist and says, "Please."

She smiles and finishes up with the little boy.

Looking at us, she says, "How many of you want to have something done?"

We all raise our hands.

She looks at her watch and says, "All right, but we'll have to work quickly. After all, it's Christmas Eve."

I almost forgot.

She explains all of the things that we can have done.

O.K. decides to have a bloody scar down the right side of his face.

While she works, the makeup artist explains what she is doing.

"I use morticians' wax, what they put on dead people to beautify them," she informs us.

"Gross," I say.

"Cool," O.K. says.

Rolling the wax up to look like a worm, she then smoothes it on the skin. Next moisturizer blends the edges and then a make-believe incision is made using the end of a brush. She makes it kind of jaggedy so that it looks like a knife or bottle wound. Then she makes it look bruised. Finally, she adds the blood.

It looks so real.

It's gross.

It's scary.

Emma is next.

She gets a "black eye" and a missing tooth.

Colin gets the exact same thing done to him that O.K. had done. Now they are not only the Boring Twins. They are the Bloody Boring Twins.

I get aged because I don't want to look bloody. Lines all over my face. Powder in my hair to make it look white.

When she's done, I stare at myself in the mirror and start singing the Beatles song "When I'm Sixty-four."

Frank, who is now in the chair, says, "Don't worry. I'll still love you when you're old."

While she works on Frank, I say to the makeup artist, "How did you learn to do this?"

Looking up from the "bullet hole" that she is putting in the center of Frank's forehead, she explains, "I've studied casualty photos and gone to the police station to get gory pictures. It was very disturbing at first but it does look realistic, doesn't it?"

I look at all of us and nod.

It looks so real.

And gory.

Finally we are all done.

I smile at the makeup artist and say, "Thank you so much. And Merry Christmas."

O.K. starts singing, "We wish you a Merry Christmas."

And we all join in.

They sing.

I go "Do-wah. Do-wah."

She just keeps smiling.

Other people walk into the makeup room and join in the singing.

Soon we are singing several carols.

It's beginning to feel a lot like Christmas.

That's how I feel and that's a line in a song that we sing.

I am happy . . . I am tired.

Even if I didn't have the aging makeup on, I'd probably have bags under my eyes.

I look in the mirror at all of the Serendipities.

We look like we've been in a major disaster.

Then I look at my watch. "Time to go."

We wave good-bye and leave the museum.

It's getting dark outside.

Some people look at us but say nothing.

O.K. and Colin pretend to be dueling.

I tell them to stop fooling around, that we have to get back.

"Whatever you say, Granny." O.K. bows.

"Be respectful to your elders," Frank cautions.

I get annoyed until I remember that I have bags and wrinkles on my face, and my hair has turned white.

Even without the makeup artist, I probably would have ended up looking like this from having to be the "adult" in the group.

Making my voice sound old and crackling, I point to the boys. "You young whippersnappers. You better be good. Back in the old days, you would never have gotten away with all of this. It would have been off to the Tower of London and off with your heads!"

Everyone laughs.

We rush for the Underground, enter, go down the elevator, and wait for the train.

Some of the passengers are carrying Christmas trees.

People stare at us strangely for a split second and then look away.

If we looked like this in a New York City subway,

people would look right at us and say things like "Are you all right?" "Riding the subway is getting really rough," or "Hey, you all know you're bleeding, except for Granny over there?"

O.K. and Colin sit next to each other and pretend to be mortally wounded, close to death.

People ignore them.

I am one of the people ignoring them, which is hard because every once in a while, one of them looks directly at me and says, "Couldn't you have just spanked us?"

Frank whispers into my ear. "My darling, where has the time gone? Just yesterday, you looked so young and beautiful."

I grin at him, try to ignore the fact that he has a bullet hole in his forehead, and give him a kiss.

When we stop, he teases, "Cradle snatcher."

I grin back. "Lighten up, sonny. Nowadays lots of older women are dating younger men. You need a younger woman like you need a hole in your head."

People keep getting on and off our train. Many of them are carrying shopping bags.

It really is almost Christmas.

"South Kensington. Our stop is coming up," Emma announces.

We stand up, get off the train when it gets to the station, and go upstairs.

I wonder what everyone in the house is going to say when they see us.

CHAPTER
ELEVEN

We've been mugged." Colin and O.K. run into the house screaming.

The grown-ups come running into the living room.

Colin and O.K. hold the sides of their faces, where the scars are. Some of the red blood makeup comes off on their hands.

Emma, with her black eye and missing tooth, does a death swoon on the carpet. She is careful to keep her mouth open so the gap between her teeth is easily seen.

"I've got a little headache," Frank says, pointing to the bullet hole in the middle of his forehead.

My mother puts her hand over her heart, gasps, and cries, "My babies. My poor babies. I'm so scared. What fiends have done this to you? I'm never going to let you out of my sight again, not for this vacation, not forever."

Now THAT is scary.

My father looks at me. "The fright has aged our beloved daughter. Now she looks like my mother."

Now THAT is really scary.

Aunt Judy rushes up to the kids, steps over Emma and "examines" O.K. and Colin's wounds. "We'll rush you all over to the emergency room and get you tetanus shots. They are ever so painful, but necessary."

My father says, "If you don't live, to whom should we give your Christmas presents?"

Trevor laughs.

I look at the grown-ups, put my hand on my hip and ask, "So how did you know?" Aunt Judy grabs Emma's hands and pulls her up from the floor. "I knew that you were going to the Theatre Museum. My students had all of this done to them when they went there so I figured you would too. So I warned everyone."

"Traitor." I grin.

She grins back.

"It's almost dinner time." My mother looks at her watch.

"Frank, darling, we brought a change of clothes here for you," Mrs. Lee says.

Almost dinner already . . . Christmas Eve . . . . . I was hoping that Frank and I could have some time alone together.

No such luck.

We all head upstairs to clean up.

Frank gives me one fast kiss before he goes into the boys' room to change.

Emma and I go into our room.

She takes something out of the closet and comes up to me.

"Do you think this is a good dress to wear to dinner tonight?" Emma holds up a pretty purple dress.

I nod. "It's very nice. You'll look wonderful in it."

She sits down on the edge of my bed and looks at the dress. "Mum gave it to me. I was going to wear it to a party that she was going to take us to on Boxing Day."

"You must miss your mom at Christmas," I say.

She nods and smiles. "I do . . . . . but I'm having fun here. You'd like my mum. She's really nice."

I smile back. "Maybe someday I'll get to meet her."

She nods and grins. "Kendra, that would be great. And I know that she would like you."

I smile at her. "I'm glad that you're here, that we're getting a chance to know each other like this. I'm sorry that your grandmother is so sick, but I'm glad that it's worked out so that we've met."

She just keeps smiling at me. "So you like me?"

I nod and smile back.

She continues, "I was afraid that you were mad because you couldn't be in my room alone and because Colin and I are always around you and Frank."

Looking at her, I shake my head. "No . . . I'm not mad that you're here."

I think about what she's said about it being her room.

I never really thought about that.

Since I got here before Trevor picked the kids up, I've sort of thought about it as my room.

Maybe that's because Aunt Judy and Trevor recently moved in and Emma hasn't had a chance to really fix it up in her own personality.

Then I continue. "Sometimes Frank and I don't want all of you around, but it's not personal. We just want a chance to be alone together."

I pick out a scarf to wear in my hair.

Softly, she says, "Did you ever want to have a sister?"

"One little bratlet factoid brother is quite enough," I joke.

And then I look at her face.

She looks sad.

"I remember when I was little, before O.K. was born, I wanted a little sister. And then I kind of got used to him and thought that I liked being the only girl and the older sister, so I didn't think about having a sister anymore."

I pause for a minute. "But if I did have another sister, I would want her to be just like you."

"Really?" She looks so happy.

I nod.

And then I think about what I said. At first I said it only because I knew it would make her feel good, but I realize it's true.

"We can pretend we're sisters," she says.

"All right. It's a deal."

She watches as I put on my makeup.

I put a little light-pink lipstick on her.

She just keeps smiling.

We go downstairs.

Frank is waiting for me at the bottom of the steps.

He's in a suit.

He looks so grown-up.

And so cute.

He always looks so cute.

"Kendra." He holds on to my arm. "Before you go in, I need to see you . . . . alone."

Emma looks up at us. "I can take a hint. Sisters can take a hint."

She's smiling so I don't think she's upset.

Frank rushes me into the laundry room and gives me a big kiss.

We seem to be spending a lot of time kissing around appliances.

"I wanted to give this to you tonight. I didn't want you to open it in front of everyone." He hands me a little jewelry box.

"Your presents are upstairs."

He makes a face. "Don't worry."

I unwrap the present and open the box.

Inside is a silver heart on a chain.

Our names are inscribed on it.

"Let me help you put it on."

I hand him the silver heart and as he puts the necklace on me. "I've already given you a heart, my heart." I can't believe that I've just said that. If I heard someone say that on TV, I would make fun of them for saying something so goopy and romantic.

But I mean it.

And then I tell him that I love him.

And he tells me that he loves me.

And then my father yells out for us.

I'm never ever going to forget this Christmas Eve . . . . . . not ever.

CHAPTER

TWELVE

Dear Bethany,

  I can't believe that you left that message on Aunt Judy's message machine. "Tell Kendra that we want ALL the news or she's dead meat." Don't the rest of you have a life back there in the Big Apple?

  There's not much to report.

  And there's not much time to report it because soon we're going to a pantomime.

  Here's a brief report.

  I love Frank.

  We never have any time alone.

  I am being driven nuts by the scavenger hunt.

  I've decided to send you excerpts from the log that will tell you what we've been doing. (Trevor let me use his copy machine and I've cut out some of the best of the Serendipity entries. I am also sending you a copy of a picture of my rear end since I sat on the copy machine and took a picture of it. I am wearing my new denims in case you can't tell.)

Anyway, here are some of the entries:

CHRISTMAS EVE:

Trimming the tree was fun. (Kendra)

Colin threw the tinsel in large clumps but I fixed it. (Emma)

I ate more popcorn than I strung on the tree. That almost made me sick. (O.K.)

When they said to put the angel on top of the tree, I tried to put Kendra up there. (Frank)

Frank's saying that really almost made me sick. (O.K.)

CHRISTMAS DAY:

EACH SERENDIPITY IS ALLOWED TO LIST HIS OR HER FAVORITE PRESENT.

My favorite is a new Nintendo from my father and Judy. I also liked the Nintendo discs that the Kayes brought me from America, where they are much cheaper. (Colin)

I love the certificate to get my ears pierced from Dad and Judy. I also love the pair of earrings that my mum gave them to put under the tree . . . . . . that was a real surprise. (Emma)

I can give you a certificate to get your brain pierced. (Colin)

My favorite is the picture of the new computer that is waiting for me back in New York. I've already named it Fido because it bytes. (O.K.)

I love the heart locket from Frank. (Kendra)

I'm glad that he didn't give her a liver locket. (O.K.)

Don't joke about my locket, brother, or I'll tell them what you called your old computer. (Kendra)

The clock is great, but I really like the sweater that Kendra gave me. It's warm and comfortable and it looks good . . . just like Kendra. (Frank)

Barf. (O.K.)

Double Barf. (Colin)

BACK TO THE CHRISTMAS DAY REPORT—WE ATE. WE PLAYED GAMES (CHARADES). AND THEN WE HAD A LITTLE TIME FOR OURSELVES.

********Note from Kendra to Bethany********

I'll discuss the above in more detail when I call.

BOXING DAY . . . . . THE DAY AFTER CHRISTMAS

I was very confused. I thought that Boxing Day was the time when people put on gloves and hit each other . . . like watching football games on Thanksgiving. But that's not what it is. In the old days, it was the day to give the presents to the servants. (Kendra)

Boring. It's a holiday so practically everything is closed and we couldn't do much on the scavenger hunt. (Colin)

Just a thought . . . . . . We're doing this scavenger

hunt . . . Does anyone remember hearing what the prize was . . . if there is a prize? (O.K.)

Hmmmmmmm. Interesting. (Frank)

———

"Hurry up, Kendra," my mother calls upstairs. "We're almost ready to go."

I jump up from the bed.

I've got to get dressed-up for the pantomime.

I take the curlers out of my hair and try a new style that I practiced with the gang before I left . . . . . it's the wild and fluffy look.

I put on the makeup that Bethany gave me for Christmas.

I want to look special tonight.

It's almost going to be like a date for Frank and me.

When Aunt Judy and Trevor originally bought the tickets for the pantomime, Emma and Colin were not going to be with us.

When they found out that the kids would be there, two more tickets were bought, but not in the original row of seats.

When I found that out, I begged for Frank and me to get the new tickets.

So now we're going to be able to sit together, away from everyone else, on our own, as much like a real date as we're going to have on this trip.

I can't wait.

I go downstairs.

I stand in front of everyone, wearing my "new look."

Well, it's not exactly my "new look" for every day.

———

Spending that long on my hair and makeup is definitely not my style but it's my new look that I'm trying out for special occasions.

I'm wearing the dress that I borrowed from Bethany, the one that she refers to as "that hot little number." Since it was a little short on her and I'm a little taller than she is, it's a little short-short on me, but I've seen lots of pictures in magazines where models wear even shorter dresses than this black dress.

Frank just stares at me and smiles, a really big smile.

My mother's mouth is open.

Even O.K. and Colin are silent, at least for the moment.

"Kendra Kaye, I demand that you go back upstairs and put on the rest of that outfit," my father says in a voice that I am not sure is serious or kidding.

"Dad," I say, trying not to be embarrassed that everyone in the room is staring at me, "we've seen lots of women in New York dressed like this . . . people that you and Mom know and are friends with."

He shakes his head. "Women. Not fourteen-year-old girls."

"Dad." I can hear a little whine in my voice. "I'm not fourteen. I'm fifteen . . . . . and I'll be sixteen soon."

He looks at my mother and she nods.

And then she says, "Sixteen is not that soon, though."

"Lots of my friends dress like this. In fact, I borrowed this dress from Bethany, so you know she dresses like this . . . . sometimes." I'm getting annoyed.

I'm not even sure that this is a look that I want for the

rest of my life, but I'm not a little kid anymore and I want to try out different styles.

I try again, speaking softly this time. "Daddy, I'm not a baby anymore."

He gives me one of those "You'll always be my baby" looks and says, "Even a sagging baby diaper covers more legs than that."

Yuck, I think.

My mother starts to laugh. "Honey, calm down. Her dress isn't that short."

"Whose side are you on, anyway?" He turns to her and smiles, just a little.

I sneak a look at Frank, who is staring at my legs.

I feel a little self-conscious but I'll live.

In fact, I'm kind of enjoying this.

Weird . . . . but true.

"And those earrings." My father is not quite ready to give up. "Where did you get those?"

He points to the dangling jet-black and rhinestone earrings that match the six-strand necklace I have on.

"I loaned the jewelry to her," Aunt Judy tells him.

He does one of his raising his hands and sighing routines. "All right. I give up. She's not a baby anymore . . . . . but you have to admit, she doesn't even look like a teenager anymore."

"Kendra." My mother looks at me. "Are you planning to dress like this every day?"

I think about my favorite clothes, leggings and long, baggy sweaters, and shake my head no. "But I do want to try out different styles."

Both of my parents look at each other and kind of nod.

Mr. Lee looks at his watch. "What time is the pantomime starting? Shouldn't we be on our way?"

Everyone gets ready.

Coats.

Frank helps me put on mine.

I feel so grown-up.

He stands behind me and whispers, "You are so beautiful."

I know that I'm not so beautiful, that to look like this took a lot of work.

I also know that he thinks I look so beautiful because he really does care.

I don't know how I know all of this when practically a week ago, I didn't even know how to put on mascara without poking the stick in my eyeball and getting gunk all over my face.

He smiles at me.

He's wearing a dark blue suit and a light blue sweater. The color of the sweater really makes his eyes look so blue, so gorgeous.

He's also wearing aftershave lotion, a nice one, not like the awful kind that some guys wear . . . . . His smells quiet and nice, not like it's going to make you want to retch or wheeze. (Barton Bertelski wears one like that. I think it's called Eau de Bad Taste, or something.)

But Barton's not here. Frank is.

My father comes up to us.

To me, he says, "My beautiful daughter. The chariot, our van, awaits. Might I escort you?"

To Frank he says, "Don't worry. You two will be able to sit together."

We grin at him.

He grins back.

My father escorts me out of the house and to the van.

He leans over to whisper.

I pull away a little because I think he's going to lick my ear . . . . but he doesn't.

"Kendra," he says softly, "I'm not sure that I like how fast you are growing up, but I am sure that I like the person you are growing into."

"Oh, Daddy," I say and give him a hug.

Frank walks over to us.

My father looks at him and says, "She's all yours."

Frank grins.

My father shakes his head. "Not ALL yours."

I stand between them. "I am all MINE."

CHAPTER

THIRTEEN

Frank Lee. Kendra Kaye.

Frankly, I like the way our names sound together.

We are all in the van with a driver that Trevor has ordered for the evening.

Frank sits close to me, with his arm around my shoulder.

I really want to kiss him and I have no doubts that he really wants to kiss me.

There are, however, ten other people in this van.

So I just rest my head on his shoulder.

Mrs. Lee is talking about her shopping excursions and about how much she loves being in big cities.

Mr. Lee says, "Give me farm life anytime."

I think about what it must be like to be Frank, to live with people who want such different things.

I snuggle a little on his shoulder and hold Frank's hand.

We keep touching and stroking each other's palms, saying nothing.

Emma is sitting on the same row of seats as we are.

O.K. and Colin are on the row of seats behind us, hitting each other lightly and going "Splat. Splat. Splat."

They are so immature.

Trevor asks the driver to tell us about Shaftesbury Avenue, the street the theater is on.

He explains that this is a major street in the theater district and that when cab drivers learn the names of the theaters on it, they use the sentence, "Little Apples Grow Quickly, C," or LAG QC . . . . . . Lyric, Apollo, Grove, Queens, Columbia, to remember them.

I'm not paying attention to the driver because Frank is holding my left hand.

With his thumb and index finger, he makes a circle around my ring finger as if it's a wedding or engagement ring.

It's the most romantic thing that's ever happened to me.

I then do the same to him.

No one else knows what we are doing.

We look down at our imaginary rings and then we look up at each other and smile.

I've never felt so special in my life.

The van pulls up in front of the theater.

"We're here," Trevor announces. "Everyone out of the van, and inside."

Frank and I get our tickets, wave good-bye to everyone else, and head off for our seats.

Frank and I hold hands as we walk down the aisle.

I feel so grown-up . . . . out at the theater with my boyfriend, all dressed up.

It's a shame that we're going to be seeing a pantomime, people performing without a sound. I've just never liked pantomime.

Once we get seated, we talk . . . and talk and talk . . . about what we've been doing at our schools . . . about things we like . . . music, books, TV. It's so much nicer being together and talking that just writing letters.

The lights dim and darken.

Frank and I hold hands.

The orchestra starts to play, loudly.

And the pantomime starts.

I can see now that pantomime in England is not the same as pantomime in America.

It's very noisy.

And strange.

A woman is playing the Principal Boy. . . . Some guy in a dress, wig, and a lot of makeup is playing the Old Dame. He's also got huge, huge balloons on his chest. . . . Now those are implants.

And at certain times the entire audience screams and yells and boos.

At times it's almost like a circus.

People on stage start doing acrobatics.

Frank is using his fingers to pretend to be a tightrope walker across my kneecap. I think that my boyfriend is developing a fixation about my knee . . . . . . I guess he really kneeds me . . . . . .

I am sorry when the curtain comes down for intermission.

Frank and I stand up.

He's grinning and laughing and looking at me. "Are you having a good time?"

"Great."

"Me too." He gives me a little kiss on the lips.

I kiss back.

There's a tug on my arm.

It's Emma. "They want you to come back to the drinks bar. They've ordered soda for you."

I was perfectly happy to stay right where we were, but we head back.

It would have been fun for me to keep pretending that Frank and I were actually out on a date by ourselves.

When we get there it's actually fine.

It's kind of like we are all coupled up, Mom and Dad, Mr. and Mrs. Lee, Aunt Judy and Trevor, and Frank and me.

Colin, O.K., and Emma have gone to the front to buy ice cream.

It's kind of strange.

I feel very grown-up right now.

And yet I know inside of me there is still a large part of me that is still a kid . . . . . . still afraid of stuff, still not knowing enough . . . . . but it doesn't scare me the way it used to scare me.

In fact, I kind of like it.

CHAPTER

FOURTEEN

"I'm too pooped to pop." O.K. puts his head down on the table.

"Me too." Colin puts his head down on the table.

"Me three." Emma does the same.

"This museum is called the V. and A., right?" O.K. asks.

"It's short for the Victoria and Albert Museum," I tell him.

"It should stand for Very and Annoying." He opens one eye, then closes it and pretends to snore.

"Stop that." I push his arm. "I love this museum and it's not polite to fall asleep right here."

We're in the cafeteria at the museum at lunchtime.

"I could have fallen asleep walking around," Frank says. "All this touristing is getting to me."

O.K. raises his head. "We could all have taken a nap on the Bed of Ware. That bed is gigantic. What is it, ten feet square?"

Frank yawns.

Taking a sip of my tea, I say, "I love this museum. It's my favorite. I could spend the entire time in here. We've only just begun to explore it."

"Kendraaaaaa," Frank pleads, "it's the Museum of Decorative Arts . . . not my thing."

"It's my thing."

"You didn't seem too excited by the Science or Natural History museums this morning."

I shake my head. "Those were two museums I could have rushed through, but you guys wanted to spend hours there."

"I want to go to Hamley's," Colin says.

"Not on our list." I shake my head. "It's a toy store."

Then I shake my head again. "Not on our list. Not on our list."

"I am so sick of hearing that," O.K. says.

"Me too." I pat him on the head.

"I am not a dog." He grins at me.

"Do you realize how many times one of us says that we've got to hurry up to go to the next thing? I'm getting sick of hearing that too."

O.K. puts some cream on his scone and then uses some of the cream to make a moustache on his face.

Colin does the same.

It's my turn to put my head on the table.

They are driving me nuts.

I want to see the jewelry room here, and they don't.

I want to look at the clothing exhibit, and they don't.

Frank looks at his watch. "Speaking of rushing to the

next thing, I want to see the Tower of London today."

"Let's stay here," I plead.

The younger boys make retching sounds.

They are driving me crazy.

I try to ignore them and mentally start listing some of the ways they have driven me nuts lately.

They tried to make the guards at Buckingham Palace laugh by yelling jokes at them. (Actually I liked one of Colin's jokes. He made a royal wave with his right hand and then asked, "Why doesn't the Queen wave with this hand?" and then he answered, "Because it's MY hand." ...... Maybe you had to be there, but I thought it was funny.)

When we went to Westminster Abbey to do Brass Rubbings, O.K. said that he would like it better if we had taken the BR off brass.

They kept complaining because the Elgin Marbles were not the kind of objects that are in a Chinese checkers set. I could have told them that the Marbles were statues.

"Kendra." Frank touches my shoulder. "Come back to Earth. You aren't listening. We're ready to go to the Tower of London."

I look at Frank, my cute Frank, Frank who is always saying how much he loves me ...... and I say, "I want to stay here."

"Oh," Colin and O.K. moan.

"I want to go." Frank stands up. "We'll never get to everything on the list."

I stay seated.

Frank folds his arms across his chest. "We have to go. There's not a lot of time left."

"I want to see the jewelry." I fold my arms across my chest.

Neither of us moves.

Emma starts to cry.

She's never done that before.

Frank kneels down next to her.

I touch her arm. "What's wrong, honey?"

She looks at both of us. "I don't want you to fight. I hate fighting. Mum and Daddy used to do that."

"It's okay," I say, and then realize it's not.

We are fighting.

But there's a reason.

No one says a word for a few minutes and then Frank sits down at the table.

"Kendra, this is scary. We're starting to act like my parents do . . . disagreeing, not wanting to do what the other one likes to do."

We are silent for a few minutes, and then I smile at him. "There are some things we like to do together."

He smiles back.

"Like kissing," O.K. says, and then makes little puking sounds.

"Like kissing," I say softly, looking at Frank. "And there are places that we have liked going together."

Colin joins O.K. making the puking sounds.

Frank looks at them. "Cut it out. We're talking. This is serious."

They look surprised.

Frank never talks to them like that.

I'm glad that he did.

I get tired of always being the strict one.

We all sit quietly for a while and then I say, "Let's work this out. It's hard. We're spending all our time together, all five of us. And the hunt isn't fun anymore. There's so little time and we all like different things."

"I've got an idea." O.K. raises his hand.

"We're not in school. You don't have to raise your hand." Frank grins at him.

"Boys do everything together. Girls together."

"Kendra and I want to spend time together," Frank tells him.

"So what do we do?"

I think for a minute. "Today, we compromise. Tomorrow, we make some changes."

"No scavenger hunt," O.K. says.

"No log," Colin contributes.

"No more fighting." Emma looks at us.

"I have a plan." I grin. "First let's see the jewelry. I'll see the costumes another day. And then we'll go to the Tower of London . . . . . and then tonight, when our parents go to that play—we'll plot it all out."

"I love plots," O.K. says.

We get up, clear our trays, and head out.

While we look at the jewelry, I find myself thinking about lots of things . . . . . how I love Frank and want to spend time with him, even though in a lot of ways we are very different . . . . . . how I hate the fact that he lives halfway across the country and that makes it hard to be real boyfriend and girlfriend. . . . . I want more. . . . I want to have a boyfriend who I can get to know day by day, not just for vacations. . . . I'm really going to miss him when this vacation is over. Without him, how am I ever going to enter the Olympic Walking and Kissing Marathon?

I think about Frank.

I also think about all of the other people in my life, how I never want to turn into one of those girls who makes her boyfriend her whole life.

Life sure does get complicated when you get older.

"Kendra, are we ready to go yet?" O.K. tugs at my sleeve.

I nod.

He says, "I've been thinking. I've got a great idea about what we can do to convince our parents to give up on Serendipity Winter."

"Me too." I give him a high five.

We leave the museum and walk down a side street.

"Kendra, look at this!" Frank is pointing at a plaque by the side of the V & A.

I read, " 'The damage to these walls is the result of enemy bombing during the Blitz of the Second World War 1939–1945, and is left as a memorial to the enduring values of this great museum in a time of conflict.' "

We all look at the damage.

It's amazing, like a history lesson coming to life.

I think about how glad I am that this museum wasn't more damaged, and I start to understand what happened to London during the war.

Maybe we *should* all go to the Cabinet War Rooms, where the war effort was plotted out.

But for today, it's off to the Tower of London . . . and then, a plot of our own.

CHAPTER

FIFTEEN

So tell us about your trip to the Tower of London." My mother smiles at us.

I hope that she's still smiling after our announcement.

I also hope that Trevor gets off the kitchen phone soon, so that we can make the announcement. I don't see why he has to take a business call on his vacation.

The living room is filled with the regular cast of characters.

Mr. and Mrs. Lee are sitting on the couch not looking very happy, but then they never do.

Emma is in a chair, grinning at me. She's glad that we're going to be spending a day together—just us.

Aunt Judy is sitting on the edge of the chair, holding a cup of coffee with one hand and ruffling Emma's hair with the other.

My aunt's wearing another outfit that I would love to borrow, black stretch pants and a black sweater, with a very colorful design that looks like it was painted by Matisse, this painter whose work I really like.

Easily, I could spend one whole day of this vacation, if we had more time, trying on her entire wardrobe.

My father is standing next to my mother, with his arm around her waist.

Frank is standing next to me, with his arm around my waist.

O.K. and Colin are sitting on the floor.

Colin starts first. "I liked all of the towers, especially Bowyer Tower, where the instruments of torture are kept."

That figures since sometimes Colin can be an instrument of torture.

"I was hoping that they sold thumbscrews in the gift shop. But they don't," O.K. says, and then adds, "I did some research about Beefeaters. I asked the Beefeater who was our tour guide if he ever ate lunch at the McDonald's across the street from the Tower . . . . . . food like 'Off with Their Head McNuggets' or 'Moat McMunchies.' "

"He was so embarrassing." Emma shakes her head.

O.K. sticks his tongue out at her and grins.

She does the same to him.

"I love the place where the Crown Jewels are kept." I pretend to put a crown on my head. "But they wouldn't let me try any of them on. I especially liked the small crown of Queen Victoria."

"A niece with simple tastes," Aunt Judy jokes.

"I was very interested in something that the Beefeater who led our tour said," Frank says. "It's about the ravens."

He pauses a minute.

"There's a legend that if the ravens who live there leave the Tower, the Tower and the kingdom will fall. So their wings are clipped so they can't fly and leave."

"That's interesting," my father says.

"There's another fact that I found really interesting."

"Tell us." My father uses his teacher voice.

"Well." Frank has a funny grin on his face. "With their wings clipped, they can't fly . . . . . . and ravens mate in the air, so they can't mate."

He pauses and then says, "I can identify with those ravens."

There is silence and then Aunt Judy laughs.

And my mother starts and my father does too.

"Frank." His mother sounds shocked.

I'm a little embarrassed, actually more than a little embarrassed.

"I don't get it," Emma says.

"I'll explain it to you when you get older." Aunt Judy gives her a hug.

My father looks at Frank. "Good. You just keep identifying with those ravens."

"Daddy!" I say.

Trevor comes in from his study. "Sorry, but that was an important call. What's everyone laughing at?"

"I'll explain it to you when you get older," Aunt Judy teases and then says, "Later."

"Now that everyone's here, we, the Serendipity Five, have something to tell you," I say, quickly changing the subject.

Everyone looks at me.

I give a fast summary. "We don't want to do Serendipity Winter anymore. We don't all like the same things. We don't want to go to all the same places. We don't want to spend our vacation looking up facts. We like to be told the facts, we just don't want to HAVE to do research on our vacations . . . except for O.K., and he wants to look up the things he wants to look up, not the ones he has to."

The non-Serendipities are quiet . . . for a minute, and then my father speaks.

"I thought you enjoyed Serendipity Summer." He shakes his head. "We thought that this would be a great way for you to explore London."

"We did, most of the time." I wish that the other Serendipities would help out with this, but once more I seem to be the one in charge. "But it's different now . . . . . more people, different interests. And there's so little time left. And Frank and I want to spend a little of it together."

Frank speaks. "We're not asking for a weekend in Paris, we just want to be able to go out in public together alone."

"That's understandable." My father nods his head. "In public."

I sigh. "Daddy, you let me go out with boys in New York."

My father sighs. "That's only because your mother and I realize that dating is 'age appropriate.' However, when you do go out, we spend the entire evening worrying until you get home."

I wonder if every girl has to go through this with her parents.

I decide to continue talking about how we all want the changes to work. I explain the arrangements, who will go out with whom on which days, how tomorrow the boys will go to all of the places they want to, and the girls will go where they want to go. That way there's an older kid with each group. Then one day, Frank and I will go out on our own . . . and someone else can watch the younger kids . . . and then it'll be New Year's Eve, which everyone will spend together.

Before our parents have a chance to object, we hand them our "Oldies but Goodies Combination Scavenger Hunt and Fact-Finding Sheet."

"And," O.K. says, "you have to answer all of these questions before you leave and then you have to go to all of the places on the list, even if it's a place you don't want to go to, even if you have plans of your own."

"Excuse me, young man." Mr. Lee clears his throat. "I don't think it's appropriate for a child to be giving orders to adults."

I look at Frank.

His face looks angry and I'm afraid that he's going to say something he'll regret.

I whisper in his ear, "Let it go."

Frank shakes his head. "Dad, we're all just doing this

to prove a point. Just look at what we've done. It's fun . . . . . and we worked hard at it."

Mr. Lee looks at his only son.

Mrs. Lee puts her hand on her husband's hand.

And then Mr. Lee looks down at the Oldies but Goodies Combination Scavenger Hunt and Fact-Finding Sheet, and he starts to laugh.

In a way, it's a shame that we aren't still keeping the log.

Mr. Lee's laughter would be an event to mark down and remember.

"This took a lot of work." My father looks up from his reading.

I nod and say, "O.K. and Colin got most of the facts together. The rest of us helped to organize the questions and figure out which places to send you that would most not meet your interests. And then we all decided that you would ALL have to do everything that's on the list TO-GETHER."

"You've done a great job," Trevor says. "Now, Colin, if only you would put this much time into your school-work."

Colin crosses his eyes.

"Your point is well taken," Mr. Lee says. "I don't like being told how to spend my vacation, and I definitely wouldn't want to spend the entire time with a large group, not under the best of circumstances."

Mark this down in our log, I think.

My father looks at my mother, then Aunt Judy, Trevor, and the Lees.

It's grown-up telepathy time.

And then he looks at us, the Serendipities.

"I would like all of you kids to go into the kitchen while the rest of us hold a conference to consider your request. We'll call you back into the room as soon as we make a decision."

We all go into the kitchen.

"Let's see if there are any Ring Dings left." O.K. brought his own supply of his favorite food with him since Aunt Judy had written and told him that they weren't sold in London.

He finds the box under the kitchen sink.

We each eat a Ring Ding . . . . and wait.

CHAPTER
SIXTEEN

We've won.

We have done it.

We had a problem.

We figured out what to do.

We did it.

Our parents listened.

There are, however, a few provisos. (That's what my father calls them, "provisos." I would call them "rules, restrictions, warnings.")

The people in each of the two groups must stick together within that group. The subgroups are now to be called the Serendipity Two and the Serendipity Three.

Frank and I, when we are together alone, are now also to be called the Raven Two and we have been told never to forget that.

I personally wish that Emma would stop saying "I don't get it," when ravens are mentioned.

Aunt Judy brings out a huge pot of tea.

She's also brought out "biscuits," cookies to Americans.

Trevor carries in cans of soda.

We all settle down with our snacks.

"Now." My father grins. "I think it's time to look at what our children are doing to us."

THE
OLDIES BUT GOODIES
COMBINATION SCAVENGER HUNT AND
FACT-FINDING SHEET

created and concocted by
O.K. KAYE, COLIN ATKINSON, FRANK LEE,
KENDRA KAYE, AND EMMA ATKINSON

PART ONE—MULTIPLE GUESS

1. What fictional character lived at 221B Baker Street?
   A. Sherlock Flats
   B. Sherlock Houses
   C. Sherlock Holmes

2. How many King Henry's were there before Henry VIII?
   A. Seven
   B. Forty-two
   C. Eleven

3. Where can you stand on the Zero Meridian Line?
   A. Redwich
   B. Greenwich
   C. Slightly Tanich

4. What is sinking at a rate of 12 inches a century?
   A. The Kitchen
   B. London
   C. The Yellow Submarine

5. Who sends Britain a huge Christmas tree to put in Trafalgar Square to say thanks for help during World War II?
   A. The Christmas Tree Bunny
   B. Shrubs R Us
   C. Norway

6. Who invented the sandwich?
   A. The Lord of Liverwurst
   B. The Earl of Sandwich
   C. The King of Kippers
   D. The Lady of Ladyfingers
   E. The Baron of Bangers and Mash

7. What is the Marble Arch?
   A. The place where giants play with the Elgin Marbles
   B. Once the main gateway to Buckingham Palace, now on the northeast corner of Hyde Park
   C. A condition caused by putting marbles in your shoe

8. What is Thomas Crapper famous for?
   A. The Tommy Gun
   B. Perfecting the flush toilet (also known as the water closet)
   C. Don't ask.

9. The day's business at the House of Commons closes with the call:
   A. "Anyone want to go out for a cup of coffee?"
   B. "Anybody here ready to stop being common?"
   C. "Who goes home?"

10. The largest of London's parks (about 340 acres) is:
    A. Hyde Park
    B. Seek Park
    C. Dr. Jekyll Park

PART TWO—WHICH OF THE FOLLOWING
ARE NOT REAL ANNUAL EVENTS:

A. Clown's Service
B. Mothering Sunday
C. Toenail Biting Day
D. Hot Cross Bun Ceremony
E. The Quit Rents Ceremony
F. Oak Apple Day
G. Beating the Bounds
H. Knollys Rose Ceremony
 I. Beating the Retreat

J. Royal Ascot

K. Beating the Eggs

L. Doggets Coat and Badge Race

M. Jersey Battle of Flowers

N. Costermongers' Harvest Festival

O. Tap Dancing Down Regent Street Thursday

PART THREE—PLACES

We cannot decide which places in London you
would all hate or love to go as a group BE-
CAUSE we realize that people are individuals
and so WE would NEVER dictate what every
person will enjoy . . . . hint, hint, hint.

"We get the hint." My mother nods.

"You kids really worked at this." Aunt Judy sounds
pleased.

"It was fun," I say.

The Serendipities all grin.

It was fun.

We all looked through references books, made choices,
had discussions.

Drats.

That makes it sound like hard work, like the S word
(*school*).

But it was fun.

And what is going to be even more fun is spending the
next few days doing what we really want to do.

———

CHAPTER
SEVENTEEN

Dear Bethany,

It's making me crazy that you weren't home when I tried to call you yesterday.

I think you should stay home every moment of the vacation to be there when I call (just kidding . . . sort of).

There is SO much to tell you . . . and I didn't want to leave it all on the answering machine in case someone else listens to your messages.

And anyway, I used up all my time on the card so I'm writing all of this down because this has been the most amazing vacation, probably the most amazing time in my life, and I don't want to forget a minute of it.

Remember at Teri's, we were supposed to tell what we really wanted for Christmas and I said art books? Well, that wasn't quite true. What I really wanted was to have my parents treat me more like a grown-up, to let me make some decisions on my own, to not be so overprotective. Well, it's beginning to happen . . . . . . a little. They still have a lot of work to do on the not being so overprotective part, but two out of three's not bad. And I wanted to learn who I really am and what I really want. I still want to know those things but I'm beginning to . . . . . I think.

I've learned so much.

So much is still so confusing.

I really can't wait to talk to you in person.

I really want to work in an art museum or something like that some day.

I wish that I could be a great artist but I think my general lack of drawing talent might be a problem (A BIG PROBLEM).

It was so much fun to spend some time in the museums the way that I wanted to . . . . not being rushed or nagged.

The museums here are amazing, totally amazing.

I went to them with Emma. She's a good kid. You'd like her. She's funny and sweet and smart . . . and she thinks I'm wonderful. I told you she was smart (I'm just joking . . . not about her being smart . . . but about me being so wonderful).

I've learned some other major things too.

I'm learning that it's one thing to really like

some guy and it's another thing to actually work things out in a relationship.

There are guidebooks to get around London.

There should be guidebooks for everything.

Life is beginning to sound like a soap opera.

Will Kendra learn to draw?

Will Frank and Kendra be separated by all those states when they return to the U.S.?

Will the Lees' marriage last?

Will Emma ever stop asking what it means about the ravens (I'll explain that one when I get back)?

Will my parents ever stop thinking of me as their baby?

Will O.K. and Colin ever stop teasing me?

Will O.K. feel bereft (good word, huh? I remembered it from our eighth-grade vocabulary list), totally bereft when he goes back to being just the younger brother without his sidekick, the other Boring Twin? I really can't wait to see you.

I really don't want to leave here, though.

Why does school have to get in the way of vacation?

Did you know that in England they call playing hooky "skiving"?

It sounds like an Olympic sport . . . . . skiving . . . . . . and speaking of Olympic sports, when I see you I'll tell you all about the one I'm in training for.

———

I guess that catches you up with the basics (so, there were a lot of basics).

How are you doing?

How is Chris?

Did you ever get a part in your dad's film?

Actually, it's kind of silly to be asking you all of this since I'll probably be seeing you before you even get this letter, but I wanted to write all of this down. . . . I guess there's as much for me to understand as for you to know.

I hope you enjoy my news!

Happy News Year!

I'm going to sign off now.

It's Frank's and my day together and he's going to be here any minute.

I am so excited.

Love,
Kendra

I put the letter in an envelope, stamp it, and think that maybe I should just bring it back with me, but decide not to. Bethany loves getting mail.

There's a knock on the door.

"Kendra, it's me. Aunt Judy."

"Come in," I call out.

She sits down on my bed. "I thought I would come see you while Trevor has taken the kids out to pick up ice cream."

"Great." I smile.

She smiles back. "It's been so good to see you, spend some time with you . . . . . not enough, but it's been so busy. I know that we expected to be able to spend more time together, but with Emma and Colin here that just hasn't been possible. I wanted them to have a good holiday in spite of the changes and upset. I want to thank you for how good you are with them, especially with Emma."

"I really care about them. You really care about them too, don't you?"

She nods. "I'm at the point in my life where I didn't think I was going to have kids and now I have two, part-time, but here a lot and I love them."

"They are terrific kids."

She looks at me. "Do you really think so?"

I nod. "Colin drives me nuts in the way that O.K. drives me nuts but yes, I like him. And I think Emma is wonderful."

"That's good, because I want to discuss something with you."

I wonder if she's going to give me one of the raven lectures, like if Frank and I don't keep our wings clipped we're going to end up with a little Colin or Emma.

"You know that their mother had to go to Boston to take care of her mother. Well, we got a call last night. Joan, their mother, wants to help her mother out for a while. And she said that as long as she's there, she wants to take a little time to finish up a long-ago-started master's degree. She wanted to know what we thought about keeping Emma and Colin for the rest of the school year and for the summer."

"Doesn't she care about them?" I am shocked. I am also a little teary because I've stuck the mascara stick in my eye.

Aunt Judy nods and hands me a tissue. "She loves them, but taking Emma and Colin to the States right now, though, would be disruptive and she wants to help her mother out. They're very close and she's an only child and Trevor says she always felt a little guilty about moving so far away. Trevor also thinks that maybe there's an old boyfriend in the picture, someone that she saw when he came over here on a business trip several months ago. We're just glad that she didn't suggest taking the kids to America. It would rip Trevor apart if they lived so far away. Hopefully, she'll come back here and not want to take them away."

"How do they feel?" I worry about Emma.

"We haven't told them yet. We didn't want to ruin their vacation, their time with all of you.

"This summer, if you would like, we would love to have you come back here and live with us . . . be our *au pair* . . . . . . sort of a baby-sitter . . . help take care of the kids . . . . . we'll pay for your plane ticket and we'll pay you, give you some time off to explore the city, go to museums . . . . . . maybe you'll even want to take some art courses . . . . . . I'll even let you borrow some of my clothes. Trevor and I have already discussed this with your parents and they've agreed if you want to do it. What do you think?"

What do I think?

I think . . . . YES, YES, YES, YES, YES.

"Yes!" I nod and hug her.

She hugs back.

"Aunt Judy, I'm so excited. I can't believe it. I love you. I love Trevor. I love the kids. I love London."

We stop hugging and she looks at me, takes a tissue, and says, "Stick out your tongue."

I do and she puts the tissue on it and uses my saliva to wipe off some mascara that has ended up on my cheek.

I decide not to think about the fact that there is now spit on my face but to think instead about her offer.

"Thank you. Thank you. Now I'll really get a chance to see London and spend some time with all of you."

She grins. "Kendra, there was once a famous writer named Samuel Johnson. He said, 'When a man is tired of London, he is tired of life; for there is in London all that life can afford.' Now you know why I love it here."

I take a deep breath and try to calm down, try to think logically.

I have an idea. "Aunt Judy, why don't you ask Frank if he wants to come back this summer? He gets along well with the kids, too."

Immediately, she shakes her head. "We all thought you would ask that. No, honey. Just you."

I try my sad face.

It doesn't work.

"It'll give you a chance to do new things, meet new people."

"Are you asking me to work here to keep me away from Frank?" I am beginning to wonder.

"No, honey." She shakes her head again. "We've asked you to come because I'll be teaching summer school and I want you to be with Emma and Colin. And I love you and you're growing up and this will be one of the last times we can be together like this."

"I love you too."

"And Kendra, I know how much you and Frank care about each other, but I also know that you'll both be meeting lots of other people. You're just beginning to date, learn about relationships. It's just the beginning. It's exciting."

"It's scary." I think about how it would be great for it always to be Frank since he loves me and I don't have to go through a whole lot of worrying.

It was so much easier when I was younger.

Maybe I shouldn't have wished to be more grown-up.

The doorbell rings.

It's Frank.

And it's time for our date.

CHAPTER

EIGHTEEN

I walk downstairs.

Frank and my parents are talking.

I hope that he is not getting the raven lecture.

They're laughing so I don't think so.

I join them.

Frank just smiles at me.

"I'm ready."

"Have a good time," my father says. "Think of us while we're out with the kids. We're taking them to play Laser Tag and then we're going to eat at Planet Hollywood."

"Wow." Frank looks really interested.

I put my hand in his hand and give it a little tug.

He starts to laugh and looks at my father. "This is a trick, a plan, to make us want to spend the day with all of you . . . . isn't it?"

My father has the "I've been caught" look on his face: "Well, you can't blame a guy for trying."

"Daddy," I sigh.

My father grins and shrugs. "Parents worry. It's our job. When you were little, I had one set of worries. I developed a way to handle it. Now I have another set of worries. I'm trying to develop a way to handle them. It's not an easy job being a parent . . . . . You'll find out . . . . Just not too soon, I hope."

"Daddy," I sigh again . . . . . and blush.

My mother gives me a hug. "Kendra, if it makes you feel any better, my father was a lot like this when I was growing up . . . . . and especially when I was dating your father."

"We're home." It's Trevor and the kids back from buying ice cream.

"They've bought your favorite flavor," my father tells Frank.

"It's time to escape." I go to the closet and get my coat.

Frank helps me put it on.

"We'll be back late. Just to remind you, we are spending the day out, and then going to dinner and a movie or play . . . . so don't worry. Don't send out a search party."

"We'll be fine," Frank says.

We go out the door just as the kids come rushing in.

The boys look at us and make kissing sounds on their hands.

"I'll remind Emma to do that to you when you start dating," Trevor tells Colin.

"Never," Colin tells Trevor.

Finally, we're outside.

———

I look back at the house and start to laugh.

"What's so funny?" Frank wants to know.

I point to the blue plaque on their house. It says

THE KAYES AND THE LEES
VISITED HERE

Frank laughs. "I bet Trevor did that."

I smile.

We walk toward the tube stop.

"I can't believe that we have to go back in two days."

Frank stops walking and turns me toward him. "I don't want to talk about it. I don't want to think about it. Let's pretend that we can see each other every day, that it's just an ordinary day. Otherwise we won't have fun. We'll be so upset."

I nod.

He puts his arm around my shoulder and we continue to walk.

Into the tube . . . . out at Leicester Square.

We walk.

And we walk.

And we walk.

We look in stores.

There's a very tacky souvenir place where I get the rest of the presents for my friends . . . a ruler that not only measures things but lists the names of the kings and queens; a make-believe tiara; a pen that has a boat inside that looks like it's floating on the Thames (which I know how to pronounce).

Frank and I talk about everything.

We find out more about our favorite everythings.

I don't quite believe him when he says that his favorite color is plaid.

We walk our way over to Covent Garden.

It's fun to go back to a place that is familiar.

It lets me feel like I'm less of a tourist, more like we belong there.

A woman comes up to us.

She's selling flowers.

Frank buys me a single red rose.

He hands it to me. "I love you."

"I love you too."

We kiss.

We're getting very good at that.

In fact, we both listed that as one of our favorite hobbies, kissing each other.

Then we watch as two buskers juggle things back and forth: a flaming baton, a garbage can, a banana, and a frying pan.

"Hungry?"

I nod. "Yeah . . . . . but I like being out here and watching everything."

"Let's have a cement picnic. You wait here. I'll be back in a few minutes."

He goes off.

I realize that it is the first time I am truly alone since I got here.

I like that feeling . . . . . especially since I know that he'll be back soon.

Frank returns with a cardboard box. "Jacket potatoes."

We go over and sit on the steps of a church for our cement picnic.

Inside are what we call baked potatoes filled with cheese and beans.

They're good, especially on a cold winter day.

We watch as an artist at one of the booths face-paints people. Right before our eyes, people become lions, tigers, pirates, fairy princesses.

It's like magic.

The day feels like magic.

A perfectly ordinary magic day.

And it's not over yet.

And when it is, there is still New Year's Eve.

CHAPTER

NINETEEN

New Year's Eve.

Emma, Colin, and O.K. are in the TV room watching these really hysterical English videos, *Monty Python, Fawlty Towers,* and *Mr. Bean.*

The rest of the group—the "adults"—and Frank and I—the "sort-of adults"—are in the living room dancing to slow music.

Frank keeps stepping on my feet.

"Ouch" is not the most romantic word.

Nor are the words, "Oops. I'm sorry."

But I don't want to stop dancing.

I don't want all of this to end.

I don't want to think that by this time tomorrow, New York time, I will be back in New York City and Frank will be back in Wisconsin.

"Four more minutes until midnight," Colin yells, walking into the room.

O.K. and Emma are right behind him, wearing dumb

New Year's Eve hats and carrying those little horns.

Frank stops dancing. "I think I've decided to invent a new dance . . . . slower than slow dancing. . . . I'm going to call it stand dancing. We'll just stand here with our arms around each other."

I think that dance has already been invented. It's called hugging and holding, but I decide not to mention that to him.

"How about inventing the standing and kissing dance. In England, they call it snogging. We could call it the Snog."

"Good idea." He leans closer to me and we kiss.

"Two minutes," Colin, the Big Ben of the house, yells.

Frank and I are still kissing when it's New Year's Eve.

We're still kissing when Colin announces that it's four minutes past New Year's Eve.

And then everyone is hugging and kissing everyone else.

Everyone except for Colin and O.K., who are each yelling, "Yuck," "Mush," and "Don't you dare."

Aunt Judy and my mom kiss them anyway.

Someone starts singing "Auld Lang Syne."

We all join in.

And I think about what a great night this is, what a great vacation it has been.

And then I start with a "What-if."

What if there is never another time like this in my life?

What if.

And then I think that if there isn't one like this, there will be another different time.

I guess even my "What-ifs" are changing.
It's the end of one year.
The beginning of a new one.
I can't wait.

FACTS LIST

1. *How far is London from New York City?*
   3,458 miles
2. *When distances from London are given, what landmark is used?*
   Charing Cross
3. *Why was the landmark given that name?*
   It was a resting place for the coffin during Queen Eleanor's funeral procession.
4. *What does Soho mean?*
   Supposedly, it comes from a hunting cry, "So-ho."
5. *Where is Cleopatra's Needle?*
   Cleopatra's Needle, an Egyptian obelisk which is more than 3,000 years old, was donated to London and is located on the Embankment (the other one is in Central Park).
   What is buried underneath it?
   A railway guide, a Bible, a model of itself, twelve portraits of "twelve of the prettiest English ladies," newspapers, toys, some hairpins, and a picture of Queen Victoria
6. *Why are there blue plaques on some English buildings?*
   They commemorate places where famous people have lived.
   Name some famous Americans who are mentioned on blue plaques.
   i. Samuel Clemens (Mark Twain), author
   ii. General Dwight D. Eisenhower, U.S. President

iii. Benjamin Franklin, statesman, inventor, and kite flier

iv. Henry James, author

v. Washington Irving, author

vi. James Whistler, painter and son

7. *How did the area called Piccadilly get its name?*
Robert Baker, a tailor in the seventeenth century, made frilly lace collars called piccadills. His house was named Piccadilly Hall.

8. *What is Big Ben?*
It is the fifteen-ton bell—not the tower, not the clock.
Give seven facts about the clock tower.

i. Each of the roman numerals on the clock is two feet tall.

ii. The big hand is fourteen feet tall.

iii. The clock tower is 316 feet tall.

iv. When Parliament is in session, a light glows over Big Ben.

v. The minute hand is one square foot.

vi. There are four faces to the clock. They are twenty-three feet long.

vii. It was named after either Sir Benjamin Hall, the first commissioner of works, or after Benjamin Caunt, a prizefighter.

9. *What are the boroughs in Central London?*

i. City of London

ii. City of Westminster

iii. Kensington and Chelsea

iv. Camden

v. Islington

10. *How is English time measured?*

   With a twenty-four-hour clock. For example, 2 P.M. is 14:00 (it's called Greenwich Mean Time not because it's nasty, but just because it's standard).

   From where is it measured?

   Greenwich

11. *What are the Yeoman Warders who guard the Tower of London called?*

   Beefeaters

12. *What is 11 Downing Street?*

   Home of the Chancellor of the Exchequer

   What is 12 Downing Street?

   Office of the Government Party Whip (a person, not an instrument of torture . . .)

   Who is Downing Street named after?

   Sir George Downing—a former diplomat, civil war turncoat, and property developer

13. The Cabinet War Rooms are where people go to fight about what kind of storage to put in their houses. *True or false?*

   False. It's where Prime Minister Churchill and his staff planned the war effort. It was a secret underground headquarters (hidden ten feet below the streets of Westminster).

14. *Are the Houses of Parliament real houses? Are they apartments (flats)? Explain.*

   Parliament is the government of Great Britain. There is a House of Commons (the people are elected) and a House of Lords. Usually they are born into it, but not born in it.

15. The Royal Mews is where the monarch's cats are sheltered. *True or false?*

    False. It is the palace stables.

16. *What flies over the east front of Buckingham Palace when the monarch is in residence?*

    The royal standard

17. *Who is the Tate Gallery named after?*

    Mr. Gallery . . . just kidding.

    Sir Henry Tate, a sugar millionaire who donated his Victorian paintings and the building

18. *How did Covent Garden get its name?*

    It was the convent garden for the monks of Westminster Abbey (in the old days, convent didn't mean just for nuns).

19. *Why are the Buckingham Palace guards' jackets red?*

    Originally, to hide the bloodstains

20. *What is Speakers' Corner?*

    A place in Hyde Park where people can speak

21. *How is English currency different from American currency?*

    There are pence instead of cents, and pounds instead of dollars, and the values are different.

22. *What is a subway in England?*

    It's a passageway where people walk under roads.

    How is that different from a subway in New York City?

    The New York City subway uses vehicles to transport people underground.

    What is that kind of transportation system called in London?

    The tube

23. *Why do people in London have to pay for a television license?*

To support the two **B.B.C.** stations (British Broadcasting Corporation) also known as the Beeb COMMERCIAL FREE.

PART TWO: THE PLACES

Column A: MUSEUMS

Choose ten (including the eight starred museums). Visit and bring back the admission buttons, ticket stubs, or one souvenir, and at least one fact about it. Be sure to EXPLORE the museums.

* * BRITISH MUSEUM
* * NATIONAL GALLERY
* * NATIONAL PORTRAIT GALLERY
* TATE GALLERY
* * VICTORIA AND ALBERT MUSEUM
* * MUSEUM OF THE MOVING IMAGE
* BETHNAL GREEN MUSEUM OF CHILDHOOD
* THE DESIGN MUSEUM
* IMPERIAL WAR MUSEUM
* * THEATER MUSEUM
* LONDON TRANSPORT MUSEUM
* MUSEUM OF LONDON
* * NATURAL HISTORY MUSEUM
* * SCIENCE MUSEUM
* THE WALLACE COLLECTION
* DICKENS HOUSE
* POLLOCK'S TOY MUSEUM

Column B: THE PLACES

Choose five, including the two starred choices.

CABINET WAR ROOMS

LONDON ZOO

* TOWER OF LONDON
MADAME TUSSAUD'S
LONDON PLANETARIUM
HIGHGATE CEMETERY
PORTOBELLO ROAD
NEAL'S YARD
LONDON BRIDGE
TOWER BRIDGE
* WESTMINSTER ABBEY
ST. PAUL'S CATHEDRAL
THE LONDON DUNGEON
HAMPTON COURT PALACE (where Henry VIII spent five of his six honeymoons)
BARBICAN CENTRE

Column C: THE AREAS

Visit five of the following areas:
COVENT GARDEN
THE CITY OF LONDON
BLOOMSBURY
LEICESTER SQUARE
PICCADILLY CIRCUS
REGENT'S PARK
TRAFALGAR SQUARE
GREENWICH
THE SOUTH BANK
CHINATOWN

Column D: To Do

Choose 4:

SEE A PLAY

TAKE THE BUS TOUR

SEE THE CHANGING OF THE GUARD AT BUCKINGHAM
  PALACE

RIDE A DOUBLE-DECKER BUS

GO TO THE LONDON ZOO

STRADDLE THE PRIME MERIDIAN LINE IN GREENWICH
  (be in two hemispheres)

TAKE THE BOAT TO GREENWICH

GO TO THAMES FLOOD BARRIER

VISIT HARD ROCK CAFE

WALK UNDER THE THAMES (take the foot tunnel in
  Greenwich)

SEE THE SILVER VAULTS

Column E

The Serendipities are to continue to widen their food
horizons:

Choose 5:

MARMITE

BANGERS AND MASH

HAVE A FORMAL ENGLISH TEA WITH SCONES

KIPPERS

JELLIED EELS

STEAK AND KIDNEY PIE

BREAD PUDDING